To Joe
Wish you were here

25-JUL-17
L/1 7/19

WITHDRAWN

THE SCOTTISH DIAMOND

When actress Lizzie Smith begins rehearsals for *Macbeth*, she's convinced the witches' spells are the cause of a run of terrible luck. Her bodyguard boyfriend, Léon, is offered the job of guarding the Scottish Diamond, a fabulous jewel from the country of Montverrier. But the diamond has a history of intrigue and bloody murder; and when Lizzie discovers she's being followed through the streets of Edinburgh, it seems her worst premonitions are about to come true . . .

Books by Helena Fairfax
in the Linford Romance Library:

THE SILK ROMANCE
THE ANTIQUE LOVE
PALACE OF DECEPTION

HELENA FAIRFAX

THE SCOTTISH DIAMOND

Complete and Unabridged

LINFORD
Leicester

First published in Great Britain in 2016

First Linford Edition
published 2017

The characters and events portrayed in this book
are fictitious. Any similarity to real persons, living
or dead, or to real events, is coincidental and not
intended by the author.

A catalogue record for this book is available
from the British Library.

ISBN 978–1–4448–3292–1

Published by
F. A. Thorpe (Publishing)
Anstey, Leicestershire

Set by Words & Graphics Ltd.
Anstey, Leicestershire
Printed and bound in Great Britain by
T. J. International Ltd., Padstow, Cornwall

This book is printed on acid-free paper

1

I had a premonition, even before the plane landed in Edinburgh, that things between us were about to take a turn for the worse. The weather was not on our side. On a clear day, there would be glorious views over Scotland as the plane descended: the sea lapping the coast, the arches of the Forth Bridge rising and falling over the river, and the Highlands just visible in the north, all greens and soft greys.

But summer was over, and with the approach of autumn a low, sullen mist clung to the ground, swallowing up the aircraft as we made our descent, and creeping up to our windows as we juddered down the runway. When the doors finally opened and we made our way onto the concourse, a dirty drizzle was falling. I shivered in my thin jacket.

I had so wanted Léon to fall in love

with my home city at first sight. I stole a glance in his direction. His tanned features already seemed exotic and out of place. Although the flight had taken just a couple of hours, we were a world away from the heat of the Mediterranean.

'Welcome to Edinburgh,' I said, lifting my hand palm-up in the misty rain, trying to make a joke of it.

Léon smiled, but it was a distant smile, and one that did nothing to reassure me. He took my arm and hurried me towards the airport building, out of the chill. At passport control we were forced to split up — me to pass through the route for UK nationals, and Léon to queue with the other citizens of the European Union.

It was the first time we'd been separated for months. Just a short while previously, Léon had been my bodyguard and constant shadow as we worked together in the country of Montverrier. Now our time in southern Europe began to seem as though it belonged to another era.

We collected our bags and made our way to the taxi rank. The rain clung to my jacket and settled softly on my hair and skin. I gave the driver my address and he said something to Léon as he stowed our luggage in the boot — some dour Scots joke about the weather being '*dreich*'. Léon gazed at him blankly. This lack of understanding, more than anything, made me realise that although I was at home here, Léon was a stranger in a foreign land. As we drove through the wet streets, he stared out of the window. I'd grown used to his quiet manner as we'd worked together, but now his remoteness was unsettling.

Once we had reached my flat and shut out the grey weather, things didn't seem quite so bad. It's remarkable the uplifting effect a cosy gas fire and a mug of tea can have on the spirits. Léon sat in a deep armchair, his long legs stretched out in front of him. Although he appeared deep in thought, I knew him well enough by now to know that he was taking in every aspect of my room in detail — the tall bookcases in the alcoves; the threadbare rug I'd thrown down to cover the floorboards; the long, rain-spattered windows looking down onto the bustling Grassmarket.

'We're a long way from the Palace of Montverrier,' I said, looking round the sitting-room and seeing my flat through Léon's eyes. My furnishings had nothing of the opulence of Princess Charlotte's suite in the palace, where we'd spent the summer. My job in Edinburgh didn't pay a great deal — I owned a travelling theatre, and we performed plays for schools and young offenders' institutions — but I'd tried to make the most of what little I had, covering the shabby sofa with bright hand-made cushions and decorating the walls with old theatre posters.

Léon brought his gaze to mine and smiled at me. This was the smile I'd fallen in love with, the first time I saw it. 'You have a lovely room.' He placed his empty mug on the coffee table and stood. Léon is lean, but his shoulders are broad, and his presence filled my familiar room.

He moved over to the window and looked down into the busy streets below.

'So many people,' he said. 'It reminds me of Rome.'

Although Léon's father was from Montverrier, his mother was Italian, and he'd spent his teenage years in Rome. I felt a stirring of hope that perhaps he could fit in here in this busy city, after all.

'Let's go for a walk,' he said over his shoulder. 'You can show me the sights of your home town. And I can try and understand some of your barbarian Scottish accent.'

Although the last words were said lightly, I noted the tension in those broad shoulders as he stood in the grey light of the window, and I assumed he was worrying about how he'd find employment. The Montverrian royal family had paid him well to act as my bodyguard during the summer, but now our work at the palace was over, and Léon's savings wouldn't last forever. Although I earned enough to pay the rent on the flat, Léon would be far too proud to accept my support. Besides, he was a man who needed to keep active, and what would he do all day, cooped up in my tiny rooms?

The wind drove a spatter of rain against the window and rattled the chimney. Despite the warmth of the gas fire, a small chill lodged in my bones. Our time together in the glorious Mediterranean sunshine was well and truly over.

2

The start of the new school term was fast approaching, which meant I needed to start preparing for my theatre classes. While I would sit at my desk by the window in the warmth of the sitting-room, Léon would go out alone to familiarise himself with the city and to look for work. It continued to rain every day.

Soon after arriving home, the fake tan I'd been given in the Mediterranean began to fade, and my freckled Celtic complexion to return. Whilst in Montverrier I had been made up to look exactly like Princess Charlotte. It had been my job to act as her stand-in, and so my hair had been straightened and turned a honey-blonde, and my eyebrows arched and dyed black. But now my unruly auburn curls were beginning to reassert themselves, and my brows quickly lost their plucked haughtiness.

One day Léon returned from his explorations, his features glowing with the Edinburgh chill, to find me bent in concentration over my lesson plans. He stepped up behind me and took one of the curls at the nape of my neck in his fingers. He tugged it gently. 'Haud yer wheesht, my wee Scots lassie.'

I turned at his touch and lifted my face to his, eyes wide with amusement. 'Haud yer wheesht? Wherever have you learned that expression?'

He raised the headphones attached to his iPod. 'I've been learning Scottish, ken.' He broke into a grin, and I smiled back, relieved to see him joking. Léon's smiles had become more and more infrequent since we'd arrived, but I should have known he would waste no time trying to get to grips with the language. He already spoke fluent French and Italian, plus the language of Montverrier — a thick, guttural dialect almost impenetrable to anyone else except the natives. I had every confidence he would apply his dogged determination to mastering the

Scots accent.

And yet after that afternoon, and during the days that followed, Léon appeared more and more withdrawn. I'd always known him to be quiet, but now I felt a tension in the room when we were together that had never been there before. The old me would have asked outright what was wrong, but the truth is I was frightened of discovering the truth — that he bitterly regretted coming to Edinburgh and he didn't love me enough to want to stay. During the day there was a thin sheet of glass between us, keeping us apart. At night, though, it was different. Our barriers melted — but even then, there was an intensity to Léon's love-making that was new, as though each time were going to be our last.

Just a short time previously, our relationship had seemed full of endless promise. In the heat of the Mediterranean, with the glorious blue sky above us, and all through the star-filled nights, I'd fallen in love with Léon with all my heart and soul. I'd thought my love might be enough.

Now a small voice inside me whispered that perhaps it wasn't.

3

The play I was producing with my theatre group did nothing to lift my sense of unease. One evening, as I sat beside the fire memorising my lines, I must have actually sighed aloud as I turned a page.

Léon lifted his head. 'What is it, Lizzie?'

I lifted my book to show him the cover, which showed a mist-filled wood and a gloomy castle in the distance. 'I'm trying to learn the witches' spells from *Macbeth*. It's part of this year's syllabus, but I hate it. All those gruesome murders and curses.'

Perhaps I sounded overly dramatic. Léon gave me one of his rare smiles. 'I expect the children will love it. It's full of murder and magic and wickedness.'

'It's full of wickedness, all right. It's well known the play is cursed. For us actors, it's a nightmare. We have to remember not to say the name 'Macbeth' in rehearsals, because if we do, something terrible is bound to happen. We have to call it 'the Scottish play' instead. And if any of the actors forget, they have to go outside the rehearsal room, turn round three times, and knock on the door to be let back in.'

'Witches and spells,' Léon teased. 'You Scots need some sunshine to drive away your superstitions.'

I gave him a twisted smile and returned my attention to learning my lines. It was like Léon to be pragmatic, but rumours of accidents and mishaps clung to this play like no other. I couldn't help thinking that having to perform it just now was an ill omen, on a par with everything else. Nothing had been right since we'd arrived in Edinburgh.

Then Léon said, 'Do you know how we say 'break a leg' in Italian?' I shook my head, and he told me, '*In bocca al lupo.* It means 'In the mouth of the wolf.' And if ever someone wishes you good luck in this way, you must never say 'thank you', because that is guaranteed to bring you bad luck. You must answer only *crepi il lupo*. It means 'to hell with the wolf''.'

This was the Léon I knew — the one who would say 'to hell with the wolf' in such a fearless fashion. He smiled, his eyes twinkling at me, and it was such an apt reply for him, I couldn't help but laugh.

But the days that followed only increased my belief that we were being dogged by bad luck which tested even Léon's resilience.

There is a Scottish bank based in Edinburgh that sponsors a major football tournament, and they'd advertised for security staff to guard the silver trophy when it toured the grounds. It seemed a job tailor-made for Léon. He applied for the position and got through to the interview stage, and I was sure he would be offered the job.

Two days before the interview, Léon received a letter. We were sitting at breakfast. He opened the envelope and studied the contents in silence for a while. Then he stood with a strange look on his face, folded the letter and stuffed it in his pocket. He made his way to the window to look out at the street below, leaving his breakfast untouched.

'The people at the bank have decided not to interview me for the job,' he told me.

I frowned, hardly able to believe it. 'I don't understand,' I said. 'The interview was all arranged.'

He was standing with his back to me. I saw his shoulders lift in a shrug. 'Perhaps they've already found someone.' I began to protest that surely it wasn't right to arrange an interview and then reject him without even seeing him, but he said quietly, 'Just leave it, Lizzie. There will be other jobs.'

Only it seemed there weren't any other jobs. Léon applied for three more routine security jobs, and was turned down for every one without an interview. He was well qualified. It didn't make sense. Maybe I was being fanciful, but I remained convinced the curse of *Macbeth* had something to do with it, and I wished

I'd never taken the play on, no matter what the syllabus required.

One night, after a long day trying to memorise the lines from the play, I lay beside Léon, my head on his chest, listening to his thrumming heartbeat subsiding. The rise and fall of his chest lulled me, and I was drowsy, on the verge of dropping to sleep, when all of a sudden the witches' cackling voices entered my head from nowhere. *'Fair is foul, and foul is fair, Hover through the fog, and the filthy air!'*

My heart slammed against my chest. I knew it was foolish, but try as I might, for a long time I couldn't rid my mind of their words. It seemed like a warning, and I tossed and turned before finally falling into a deep, dreamless sleep.

I woke the next morning to find the rain had finally stopped, and the sun's rays were edging through the slats in the blind in the bedroom. I blinked, hardly able to believe the golden light that was drifting into the room. Léon had said we Scots needed some sunshine to drive away our superstitions, and now here it was, as if by magic. The day promised those lovely clear blue skies that could be such a delight in Edinburgh.

Léon was lying with his broad back to me. I flung my arm around his shoulder and pressed my cheek to the warm skin between his shoulder blades, my bad night's sleep forgotten.

'The sun's out,' I said. 'Did you arrange it?'

He caught hold of my fingers as they curled round his chest, and kissed them. 'Yes. Especially for you.'

I smiled into the warmth of his back. 'What will you do today?'

There it was again — that infinitesimal stiffening of his muscles under my touch, as though he were steeling himself against the rigours of another day. But he answered coolly, 'I have an interview at an agency this morning.'

'That's good,' I said brightly, although we both knew that nothing good had come of these interviews so far. Neither of us spoke for a couple of seconds. Then

I said, 'Would you like to meet me this afternoon, after I've finished rehearsals? We could take a walk around the city. Make the most of the sunshine.'

He turned and kissed me, his lips warm on mine. 'That's a nice idea,' he said.

He was smiling, and the tension in my shoulders dissolved. I threw back the covers. 'Great,' I said. 'Me first in the shower.' He laughed, aiming a pillow at me.

I made my way to the bathroom, and then I remembered I'd left my hairbrush on the dresser. When I turned back, Léon was gazing at the ceiling, his hands behind his head. He caught sight of me and looked away, swinging his legs out of the bed. 'Hurry up,' he threatened, 'or I'll be coming to join you in that shower.' It was jokingly said, but I'd caught the look on his face when he'd thought himself alone.

Later, as I stood under the warm spray, I thought of the emptiness I'd witnessed there, and I was filled with dismay. I closed my eyes, but the witches' spell leaped again into my mind, and despite the warmth of the water, I shivered.

4

Our rehearsals for *Macbeth* that afternoon didn't go well. The session finished later than I'd anticipated, and so afterwards I ended up having to speed-walk down Princes Street and then half-run up the steep stone steps of Calton Hill, where Léon and I had planned to meet. The sun had continued to shine all day, and by the time I reached the top of the stairs I was red-faced and panting for breath. During the six weeks I'd spent confined in the princess's suite with Léon during the summer, I'd had little opportunity for real exercise apart from some yoga. I found I was more unfit than I realised.

I bent double, resting my hands on my knees, waiting to regain my breath. A couple of swarthy men in dark suits approached, and as they passed one of them made a comment, and they both laughed. I lifted my head with a start. I hadn't understood the words, but there was no mistaking the guttural language. Those men were from Montverrier!

I whirled round to see them striding away down the stone steps, their backs towards me. They were talking loudly, and although I didn't understand their harsh-sounding conversation, as they descended the stairs with heavy footsteps I thought I made out the words 'Léon Bressac'.

Léon! What did those sinister-looking men have to do with him?

And then one of the Montverrians turned on the steps and looked directly at me. For a couple of seconds our gazes held. Then his lips spread in a slow smile, and he nodded his head as though he knew me, before turning to rejoin his friend. They rounded the corner and out of sight. What did it all mean? I cursed the Scottish play. Surely here was another piece of bad luck come to dog us.

I hurried towards the stone pillars of the National Monument, looming large and black against the bright blue sky, and found Léon sitting on the great stone steps, his face lifted to the sunshine. He rose to his feet as I approached.

'What is it, Lizzie?'

I reached up and kissed him. What a reassuring presence he was.

'Today hasn't started out well,' I said. 'One of the witches said the M-word in rehearsals — ' Léon pulled away with a shake of his head. 'No, listen,' I protested. 'I know you think it's just superstition, but ten minutes after she said it, there was a call from her son's nursery to say her boy had fallen and they'd had to take him to hospital.' Léon's eyes widened, and so I added quickly, 'It turned out to be just cuts and bruises, but it's given her a scare. And so that's why I was late getting here. And then when I got to the top of the steps, who should be there but two men from Montverrier.'

He took a step back, frowning over my shoulder to where I'd entered the grounds. We'd left Montverrier never wanting to return. It was a country filled with double-dealing and skulduggery, and meeting two men from there so soon after our arrival in Edinburgh seemed more than coincidence.

I rushed on: 'I heard them talking. I didn't understand everything, but I thought I heard one of them say your name, Léon Bressac.'

Léon's lips tightened. He considered my words for a moment, his blue eyes fixed on the steps in the distance. It wasn't often Léon was uncertain, but this time he appeared thrown. Then he gave a small shrug. 'Why would two Montverrians be talking about me?' he asked. 'Perhaps you were mistaken.'

'I don't think I was,' I said. 'I'm sure — ' Then I stopped. Was I really so sure? I'd just spent the afternoon rehearsing a play filled with treachery and deception. Perhaps my imagination was going into overdrive.

Léon noted my confusion. 'Come on,' he said, with the smile I remembered. 'You've been working hard. Forget Montverrier. Let's take a break and enjoy the sunshine.'

He took my hand, and as we began to stroll around the top of the hill, stopping several times to gaze at the sights below us, I gradually forgot all about the events of the afternoon. There was the high, rugged mound of Arthur's Seat beside us, the sun glittering on the river Forth, the Palace of Holyrood, and the bustling length of Princes Street with the castle at the far end of it. In the rare sun, my beautiful home city sparkled at its very best. All in all, it was a wonderful contrast to the drab day of our arrival. And it was such a delight to show the sights off to Léon, who seemed to share so much of my joy in them, that I gradually dismissed my encounter with the men from Montverrier along with my actor's superstitions.

As the afternoon wore on, Léon shared my upsurge in spirits. The old smile continued to lurk in his eyes, and occasionally he would tease me about my Scottish accent, copying my voice exactly when I pointed out the 'darrrk hoosses' below us, or the 'wee bairrrns' playing on the grass. I hadn't seen Léon so relaxed since we'd arrived in Edinburgh.

I didn't want our light-hearted mood to end, but soon we'd made several circuits round the top of Calton Hill, and there was nothing left to do but make our way back down the stone steps and head for the crowds of shoppers and tourists thronging the streets below. It wasn't until we'd walked the entire length of Princes Street and were approaching the art gallery that I saw them again — the two dark-suited men from Montverrier who'd passed me on the steps of Calton Hill.

5

The Montverrians were some distance from us. They'd stopped to talk to a young woman seated at a stall by the gallery steps. I recognised them instantly. It wasn't just their expensive suits that caused them to stand out from the passers-by. They looked like the sort of smartly dressed men who would smile politely as they pulled out a gun and blew your head off.

I gripped Léon's hand. 'That's them,' I said in a rush. 'The two guys I told you about.'

Léon was strolling at a steady pace, apparently relaxed, but his eyes were already fixed on the Montverrians, and I realised he'd seen them well before I had. It was like Léon to notice everything about his surroundings, and he was gazing at them intently.

He returned the pressure of my hand

with a brief smile. 'There's nothing at all to worry about, Lizzie.'

That was typical of Léon — the man who was always calm about everything. All my previous foreboding came back, however, and I couldn't help feeling relieved when the two men finished their conversation and turned away, heading from Princes Street in the direction of the castle. Léon quickened his pace.

'You're never thinking of following them,' I said, striding to keep up.

He looked down at me. 'Come on. Let's find out what they're up to.' There was a determined expression on his face. I almost had to trot to keep in step.

When we reached the stall where the Montverrians had been standing in conversation, there was just time for me to take one of the young woman's leaflets as we hurried past. 'Oh, look, some of it's in French,' I said breathlessly. 'Perhaps that's why those men were so interested. Seems there's an exhibition on at the castle. Some sort of fabulous jewel.'

The enormous glittering diamond

pictured on the front of the leaflet was like something from Elizabeth Taylor's wardrobe. *'Le Diamant Écossais,'* I read aloud. 'The Scottish Diamond.' I waved the leaflet under Léon's nose. 'Do you think that's where they're heading?'

He came to an abrupt halt. *'Le Diamant Écossais?'* He examined the leaflet in my hand. 'So that explains it,' he said slowly. He gazed after the fast-moving men from Montverrier, who had entered Princes Street Gardens and were now climbing the steep path towards the castle.

'Explains what?' I stared at Léon. 'Are you going to tell me what's going on?'

'The Scottish Diamond is one of the treasures of the royal family of Montverrier,' he told me. 'It very rarely leaves the country. So I expect that's why those two Montverrians are here in Edinburgh. The exhibition is sure to attract a lot of attention.'

My heart sank at the thought of my home town being thronged with Montverrians. I thought I'd escaped that

26

country of treachery forever. Just my bad luck. Or the bad luck of the Scottish play, rather.

'Why is it a Scottish diamond if it's from Montverrier?' I asked. We'd resumed our brisk strides and were now climbing the path to the castle.

'Ah, well that's a long story. And since it's to do with the people of Montverrier, it's also a story full of bloodshed and deception.'

First the ill omen as we rehearsed *Macbeth* that morning, then the two men from Montverrier, and now a diamond with a bloody history. I'd had enough of adventure during our summer in the palace, and would have much preferred to return to the safety of my quiet flat and my books. But Léon's eyes were alight with new energy as we strode upwards, and it was obvious he was eager to discover what was going on. I swallowed my feeling of foreboding and took his hand as we carried on up the hill.

6

Edinburgh Castle is more than eight centuries old. It looms over the city on top of a dark volcanic crag, and people say it was built on the site of a shrine to the witch Morgan le Fay. For hundreds of years its dark battlements have dominated the Edinburgh skyline, a symbol of royal power. This is no fairy-tale castle, but one of military might. Whenever I pass through the imposing stonework of Portcullis Gate, I think of all the footsteps that have trodden this path before me down the ages — of the bloody battles, the royal ceremonies, of King James VI's birth here, the deaths of queens, of Oliver Cromwell's army, and of the doomed Jacobite uprising. The walls enclosing the castle bear witness to great turning points in history. It's a place to inspire awe.

Léon and I slowed our footsteps as we crossed beneath the stone gate and into the cobbled interior. The sun was lowering in the western sky, and dark shadows spread from the battlements. A few tourists were still strolling around the Argyle Battery, the row of cannon that continues to point menacingly over the city. Of the two Montverrians there was no sign.

I pulled out the leaflet again and studied it. 'They must be heading towards the Royal Palace,' I said. 'Look. That's where the exhibition will be held. In a room near the Crown Jewels.'

The usual crowds of tourists had thinned out, and so as we rounded the wide curve of the path to reach the upper castle, it was easy to spot the two men we'd been following. They were standing just beyond the arch of Foog's Gate, deep in conversation with a group of similarly dark-suited men.

I remembered from my stay in Montverrier (indeed, how could I forget?) just how reactionary the principality was. It was no surprise that the group contained no women. All the women would have been left at home in Montverrier, I thought darkly, doing the ironing and taking the men's spare black suits to the cleaners.

I came to a halt just before the gate. I had absolutely no desire to go any further. Léon pressed my hand.

'Wait for me by the One O'clock Gun,' he said. 'I'm going to talk to them.'

'Are you crazy?' I hissed.

But Léon was already under the shadow cast by the stone gate, and a couple of seconds later he emerged into the courtyard. The group of men turned as one, but I didn't wait to see what would happen next. I swivelled on my heel and made my way back down the path to wait by the gun.

And a long, knuckle-biting wait it was, too. The shadows were creeping over the city, and lights were flickering on one by one in the buildings beneath. In the distance the Firth of Forth gleamed gold in the dying rays of the sun. The scene should have been one to delight the eye. Unfortunately my heart was beating far too hard to enjoy it.

I hunched over, head bent, the collar of my jacket pulled up to hide as much of myself as I could. I had no desire to speak to any of the Montverrians if they happened to head my way. Something told me no good would come of it.

I don't know how long I waited like this — perhaps half an hour, perhaps even longer. It grew darker. In the quiet of the courtyard, under the battlements, a breeze whispered. The witches' words sprang into my head and lodged themselves there: *'Round about the caldron go; In the poison'd entrails throw. — Toad, that under cold stone, Days and nights has thirty-one; Swelter'd venom sleeping got, Boil thou first i' the charmed pot!'*

When footsteps sounded behind me, I almost leaped out of my skin. Léon stepped closer, a small smile on his lips.

'Thank God you're back,' I said. 'All sorts of things were going through my mind. What on earth have you been talking about?'

'Good news.' His eyes gleamed in the gathering shadow. 'I've got a job.'

I stood there, dumbstruck. He cocked his head to one side. 'Aren't you going to say anything?'

I tried to hide my dismay. 'Of course. It's wonderful news. Isn't it?'

There was a strange look on Léon's face. He met my gaze, his mouth turning down at the corners, and for a moment neither of us spoke.

Then he took my hand. 'Of course it's good news. Come. Let's walk down into town and I'll buy you dinner to celebrate.'

7

We made our way through the darkening streets to an Italian restaurant near the Grassmarket. I was ready with a hundred questions, but Léon refused to answer any of them until we were sitting comfortably with a glass of wine. He suggested we have steak, to remind us of those evenings we'd spent at his house by the sea at the end of the summer. When he glanced down at me with his familiar smile, for a short instant in that busy street it really was as if we were back there, just the two of us, in our own bubble of happiness. But then someone pushed past us and real life intruded, and my concerns about Léon's mysterious job bubbled once more to the surface. I found myself holding on to his hand with a grip that was too tight.

When we were finally settled at our table in the restaurant, and our meals ordered, Léon raised his glass. 'To a new beginning.'

I lifted my glass to his. 'A new beginning,' I said. 'And I wish you well in your first job in Scotland.' I put down my glass and cocked my head to one side. 'And now, will you tell me all about it?'

And so as we waited for our meal, Léon finally began to recount everything he'd been discussing with his compatriots while I had waited for him by the battlements. It turned out the men we'd encountered were indeed connected with the exhibition of the Scottish Diamond. As Léon approached, they were talking loudly amongst themselves without bothering to lower their voices. Léon had thought it odd that they were speaking so frankly in front of him. It was almost as though they wanted him to hear. But then he remembered that very few people outside Montverrier understood the language, so perhaps they merely thought it unnecessary to be discreet.

And so it was that Léon overheard them discussing the sudden and mysterious disappearance of one of their

34

colleagues. He reached for a piece of bread from the basket on the table. 'I heard one of them say how Raymond hadn't turned up that morning,' he explained. 'As their conversation went on, it became clear that Raymond's job was to guard the diamond while it was on show. They were discussing his whereabouts, and whether they should look for a replacement for him, or wait and see if he turned up. It was too good an opportunity for me to miss. I walked straight up to them and introduced myself. I explained how I'd just arrived in Edinburgh and was looking for work in security. I gave them my card, but one of them said he recognised me.' He dropped his gaze from mine and carried on quickly. 'Basically, the job is mine.'

I stared at Léon in astonishment, but he avoided my gaze and occupied himself by spreading butter on his bread.

'Léon, isn't this a bit strange?' I asked. 'A security guard from Montverrier who's in charge of guarding a priceless jewel has gone missing. You turn up and are offered the job in his place, on the basis of a brief conversation. Doesn't it seem shady to you? This is Montverrier we're talking about, don't forget. Country of double-dealing and intrigue.'

Léon laid down the knife he was holding. He still hadn't met my eyes. 'Well, as you said — this is Montverrier. They do things differently. And at least now I have a reputable job.' He finally lifted his gaze to mine, and there it was again — the hollowness I'd caught in his expression that time he'd thought he was alone.

'Léon, what is it?'

'Lizzie, I — '

We both started speaking together, and broke off simultaneously. There was a short pause.

'Lizzie — ' Léon began, only I never did find out what he was about to say. The waiter arrived, bringing our meals, and I was forced to draw back in my chair to make room for our plates. By the time the waiter had finished fussing over our wine and serving us from a steaming tray of vegetables, Léon had obviously thought better of whatever it was he'd been about to say. He picked up his fork. 'Mmm. The steak looks delicious. Almost as good as mine.'

I wasn't to be diverted. I remembered how I'd thought I'd heard those two men say Léon's name, and I wanted to make sense of it. 'What did you mean when you said they recognised you? Did they mean they know it was you who was Princess Charlotte's bodyguard?'

He laid down the fork he'd picked up and finally met my gaze. 'Listen, everybody knows everybody in Montverrier.'

'Fine,' I said, after a short pause.

He reached out over the table and took my hand. 'Please don't worry,' he said. 'I have a job. It's not much of a job, but it's a start. Let's forget our worries for this evening, and celebrate.'

I nodded and gave him a small smile. His words should have cheered me. After all, he'd done well to approach a group of Montverrians and ask for a job, and be given one immediately. But that nagging feeling that something was wrong wouldn't go away. I mentally blamed *Macbeth* for my feelings of foreboding and tried to shrug them off. Then another thought occurred to me.

'You never did tell me how a Scottish diamond ended up in Montverrier,' I reminded him. 'A story 'full of bloodshed and deception', you said. What happened?'

'Ah.' Léon placed his glass on the table. 'Now this is a tale worthy of Shakespeare.'

8

I don't know if I mentioned this before, but Léon is a great storyteller. When we'd been holed up together that summer in the palace of Montverrier, his stories had helped me keep my mind off the danger that surrounded us. He would make a brilliant actor. Now he leaned back in his chair, his long fingers around the stem of his wine glass, and I settled back in anticipation.

'It was like this,' he said. 'In the year 1745, after the Jacobite rising in Scotland had failed and Bonnie Prince Charlie had fled across the water, many of those who fought with him had to run for their lives also. Some of them went to Spain, some to France, and some to Montverrier. The Montverrian royal family were Stuart sympathisers, and the rebels were sure of finding a safe haven there. Or so they thought.

'In their rush to flee, many of the Scottish aristocrats arrived in Montverrier with only the clothes they stood up in, and as much gold and jewellery as they'd managed to stuff into their pockets. One of those aristocrats was Lord Falmire. He managed to flee Scotland with his family's precious diamond wrapped inside a handkerchief and hidden in the heel of his boot.'

'Lord Falmire,' I repeated, turning the name over. 'I'm sure there's still a Lord Falmire in Scotland today. It must be his descendant. That's right!' I exclaimed as the realisation hit me. 'He has an estate to the west of Edinburgh. He doesn't use his title much. He goes by the name of Alexander Dalgliesh. He's a great patron of the arts, and when I was a student, he often came to our shows.' I chuckled at the look of surprise on Léon's face. 'After a while in Edinburgh, you'll find everyone knows everyone.'

He smiled his crooked smile. 'Just like in Montverrier, in fact.'

'So what happened then?' I asked.

40

'Don't tell me the King of Montverrier stole Lord Falmire's diamond from him?'

Léon's smile turned down. 'Well, this is Montverrier. There has to be some skulduggery involved — only it wasn't the King, but his son, Prince Sébastien. In those days, gambling was all the rage. People would bet on anything — the fall of the dice, a horse race, even ridiculous things like how far a chicken could run. And the royal family in Montverrier loved to gamble as much as anyone.

'The story goes that Lord Falmire lost the diamond playing cards with the prince during a reception ball at the palace. It was a risky thing for Falmire to do, sitting down to play with a member of the royal family, knowing he'd brought so little money with him from his own country. By all accounts, with each round of cards the stakes grew higher and higher. Lord Falmire was an accomplished player, but even so, the notes and coins he'd brought with him from Scotland gradually dwindled away, until all he had left to play with was the diamond. He staked it on

41

one last game — and the Prince won.'

As Léon told me his tale, I could readily imagine the scenes playing out in the palace — Lord Falmire arriving in his carriage in the great cobbled courtyard, I remembered climbing the magnificent staircase under the light of hundreds of candles, and then entering the enormous ballroom filled with wigged and powdered dancers. Poor Lord Falmire. The palace was a place of deception, as I knew to my cost. I pictured hundreds of rapacious eyes turning on him as he entered the room, greed glowing in their depths like a living thing. As my actress's imagination lent life to the scene, I found myself willing Falmire to turn back, and not to enter the palace at any cost.

I caught Léon's eyes on mine, and I gave a grimace. 'Poor guy,' I said. 'He didn't stand a chance.'

Léon took a sip of his wine. 'But of course this is Montverrier. The story doesn't end there.'

His eyes twinkled in the candlelight. I may have mentioned that Léon is a great storyteller. I leaned forward. 'So then what?'

He replaced his glass on the table. 'It seems that even before that night, Lord Falmire had been showing off the diamond to everyone he knew in Montverrier. He appears to have been a bit of a braggart. It's a fabulous jewel — tinged with blue, and in the shape of a teardrop, as though wept from the eye of a goddess. They say that when Lord Falmire first showed the diamond to Prince Sébastien, he was amazed at its beauty and offered a handsome sum of money for it, but Lord Falmire refused. So of course afterwards Falmire claimed the prince had invited him to play with the sole object of winning the diamond from him.'

Léon tilted his head to one side. 'And it does seem curious. The story goes that up until that night, Prince Sébastien had rarely played at cards. He was a novice, and yet that night the cards were with him time and time again against a hardened gambler. When the diamond was won from him, Lord Falmire stood up from the card table, furious, and accused the prince outright of cheating. You can imagine the terrible scenes in the card room. To accuse a prince of the royal family in his own palace! It was unheard of. Falmire's friends caught hold of him, trying to prevent it coming to blows, but the prince was furious. He leaped up and challenged Falmire to a duel.'

'What a scandal! And what a way for a prince to behave.'

Léon answered, with the gleam of a smile, 'Well, you know us Mediterranean types. Apparently we are hot-headed.'

Since you'd rarely find a man as cool under pressure as Léon, of course I chuckled at this. 'Go on with your story,' I chided him. 'What happened next? Did they really fight?'

'Of course. Duelling wasn't outlawed in Montverrier at that time, as it was in Scotland. In fact, it was seen as a badge of honour to have one or two duelling scars. Lord Falmire accepted the challenge there and then. Seconds were chosen, and the man Falmire chose to stand by him made an attempt at reconciliation. The prince's second would have none of it. And so the prince and Falmire retired immediately to the courtyard.'

'You mean they just went outside there and then? In the middle of a ball?'

Léon's eyes crinkled at my horrified expression. He nodded. 'As I said, it wasn't against the law in Montverrier to fight a duel. The times were different then, and many men carried a sword, even to go to a ball. And in any case, who would arrest the prince?'

I shook my head in astonishment. Once more I imagined the scene — the prince and Lord Falmire descending the same magnificent staircase I'd trodden myself that summer, and then out into the cobbled courtyard. There must have been torches to light the exterior, and the guests must all have followed, dressed in their finery, their jewels glittering in the light cast by the flames. What an extraordinary scene it must have been!

'And here again we have a curious circumstance,' Léon was saying. He took a sip of his wine, a slight furrow on his brow above the rim of his glass.

'The whole thing is curious,' I told him. 'What else happened?'

'The thing was, Lord Falmire had always been a fighting man. He'd fought against the English and he knew how to handle himself. By all accounts, he was an excellent swordsman. And yet out there in the courtyard, when the seconds gave the signal, he seemed like a man dazed. It was as though his sword was too heavy for him. Still, he had an advantage, as the prince was a big man, and not very light on his feet. After a short time, Falmire managed a hit to the prince's forearm that was enough to draw blood.'

Léon drew an imaginary sword and lunged with such a desperate look on his face that I shrank back in my seat. I could just imagine the scene — the swish and clatter of the swords; the gasp of the crowd as the blood began to stain the prince's sleeve. 'And so was that it? Was it all over?'

Léon shook his head. 'Prince Sébastien

refused to yield. He pressed forward, ignoring his wound. And then everyone knew he meant to fight to the death.'

'You mean he wanted to kill him? Right there, in the middle of a ball?' My eyes were round and wide with amazement.

'Yes,' Léon said. 'As hard as it is to believe, that's exactly what happened. And after that first successful lunge on Falmire's part, the Scotsman's energy seemed to ebb away. He staggered as they fought, as though he were drunk, and after a few fierce parries he was drained and barely able to lift his sword. By the end of that night, Prince Sébastien possessed the Scottish Diamond, and its owner was dead.'

I continued to stare at Léon. Even by Montverrian standards — and this was a country with a history of centuries of intrigue — it was a dramatic story. 'If Lord Falmire was such an expert swordsman, how did he come to give way so easily? Was he really drunk?' I frowned as a possibility hit me. 'Or had he been drugged?'

Léon leaned back in his chair, placing his empty glass on the table. 'Nothing was ever proved. After the duel, the King of Montverrier expelled all the Jacobites and closed the country's borders to the Scots. The Falmire family tried to use their influence at the French court to apply pressure, but Louis XV believed Prince Sébastien's claim that Lord Falmire lost the jewel and died because he was drunk. And so the Falmire family gave up their claim, and the Scottish Diamond stayed in Montverrier.'

'Until now,' I said.

'Until now.' He frowned. 'I'm surprised Princess Charlotte has agreed to an exhibition in Scotland and allowed the diamond to come back here, within reach of Lord Falmire's heir.' Then he shrugged. 'But then perhaps the controversy has finally been laid to rest.'

I stared into my wine glass, thinking this one over. 'I wonder what the present Lord Falmire thinks about it all, now that the diamond is coming home to Edinburgh. It must be strange for him, knowing it was taken from his ancestor in such a terrible way.' I thought of Alexander Dalgliesh, the present Lord Falmire, as I'd last seen him, at an after-show party a few years previously. He was a large man, in his forties, with a receding hairline that was more than made up for by a bushy reddish moustache. His face was prematurely lined, and he had an uncomfortable way of studying people. At the time I'd put it down to social awkwardness. We actors are a loud bunch when we get together, and I wondered if perhaps he felt shy. Whatever the reason, on the few occasions his eyes met mine, I'd found something in them a little unnerving.

If Léon had wanted to distract me from my worries about his new job, he'd succeeded. I began to think perhaps it wasn't so strange, after all, to be offered the job of guarding a priceless jewel after just a few minutes' conversation. Montverrier was a country with its own rules. I stopped feeling so anxious and began to relax. The old Léon had returned and was smiling at me softly in the candlelight.

The rest of the evening passed in a warm, comfortable haze, until finally Léon signalled to the waiter that it was time for us to leave. While Léon dealt with our bill, I took the opportunity to visit the ladies'. On my return, I found the way to our table blocked by a noisy group who were waiting to be seated. I detoured round them, passing the large window looking onto the street as I did so. It was dark now, but when I glanced outside I could just make out two men standing in the shadow of the doorway opposite. The whites of their shirt fronts stood out in the gloom. I guessed they must have stepped outside from some bar or other to have a smoke, and sure enough, I caught the red tip of a cigarette rising and falling. I thought nothing of it.

Léon helped me into my coat, and by the time we'd made our way back outside, the two men were gone. We crossed the road. I was chatting to Léon, speculating on how the Scottish Diamond came to be in the Falmire family in the first place. He was listening to me speak, but as usual with Léon, at the same time he was alert to everything around him. As we passed the doorway where the men had stood, we came across a cigarette still smouldering on the pavement. I would have stepped over it and gone on, but Léon stopped still. The next minute he was crouching down, a frown on his brow. He rolled the cigarette over with the tip of his finger.

'What's the matter?' The thick smell of cigarette smoke wafted up to me. It was a sweet, distinctive smell, like the one found in certain brands of strong cigarettes in France. Or in Montverrier. I made to bend down to look, but Léon stood and extinguishing the cigarette with a quick twist of his heel.

'It's nothing.' He took my hand and we resumed our walk home. I turned my head. The cigarette lay crumpled and torn on the pavement, the tobacco spilling out. Someone had discarded almost a full cigarette, as though they'd only had time for a couple of puffs and then thrown the rest away in a hurry. But the street was empty. The only thing that could have disturbed him was us — Léon and I. I glanced at Léon, all the anxiety I'd felt that afternoon returning.

He squeezed my hand. 'It was nothing,' he repeated firmly. 'Just a burning cigarette.'

9

During the days that followed this incident, I was immersed in rehearsals, and the dark-suited men from Montverrier retreated to the back of my mind. *Macbeth* is an intense play, and after a long day of rehearsing scenes of violence and high emotion, I was often drained. It was a relief to come home to Léon, and to find the fire going and a delicious meal waiting for me.

Léon had a few days' grace before beginning work, as the exhibition of the Scottish Diamond had yet to open; but as I mentioned before, he doesn't like to remain idle, and while I was at the studio he spent a lot of time walking around Edinburgh. I wondered if perhaps Léon's days spent alone gave him too much time to think, or maybe his recent work as a bodyguard had left him hyper-vigilant — whatever it was, in those few days before he began his job at the castle, he seemed on edge.

One evening I looked up from my books to find him standing by the window again, legs apart, arms crossed, frowning down at the street below. It was as if he was on the lookout. I closed the book I was reading and went to stand beside him. Below us a few cars edged down the hill, and there were the usual passers-by muffled up against the cold. Nothing to hold anyone's interest.

'What are you looking at so intently?' I teased him. 'Are you being stalked?'

He dropped his gaze to mine immediately. 'Why? Who have you seen?'

'No one,' I said, bewildered. I pointed out of the window. 'Or, that is, loads of people. Just take a look. This street is always busy. Do the crowds bother you?'

His harsh frown softened under my concerned gaze. 'You're right,' he said. 'This is such a big and noisy city. I forget you're used to living here.'

I narrowed my eyes. Since when had Léon ever been anxious about living in a big city? He'd spent his teenage years in Rome, which was far bigger and noisier than Edinburgh. And in any case, Léon was never frightened of anything.

He must have known his answer hadn't satisfied me. After a moment's hesitation, he added, 'Sometimes when I've been out walking in the city, I've had the strange feeling I was being followed.'

'What?' I cried. 'Why didn't you say anything? And who on earth would want to follow you?'

He picked up one of my hands in both of his. 'Now this is why I didn't say anything. I didn't want you to be worrying. And you're right — who on earth would want to follow me? I'm worrying about nothing. I've just had too much time on my hands.'

I continued to frown up at him, troubled. He took my face in his hands and kissed me. 'I know what it is,' he said, his eyes twinkling. 'It's all your talk of witches and ghosts. Your Scottish superstitions are rubbing off on me and I'm seeing things in this gloomy weather that aren't there at all.' He swung me into his arms and kissed me again.

After that, Léon dismissed his vigilance as something brought on by the strangeness of his new city. And once he began his new job at the castle, he didn't mention being followed again, and in fact, all the tension he'd been showing disappeared, and he became almost his old self. He left the house with a sense of purpose that had been lacking in his previous aimless wanderings around Edinburgh. And the best thing was, he was beginning to understand more and more of our Scottish brogue every day.

I later discovered it wasn't just our Scottish way of speaking he was mastering. A few days after he started work, I was in the kitchen preparing our evening meal when I heard the front door close and Léon's light tread in the hall. Usually he went straight upstairs to change, but this evening he came directly to the kitchen and put his head round the door. His eyes brimmed with amusement. I stepped closer to give him a kiss, and he pushed the door wide. My mouth fell open. He was dressed in a kilt. The green tartan cloth was thrown over one broad shoulder in Highland fashion, and the pleated skirt revealed an inch or two of tanned, muscular leg above a pair of thick cream-coloured socks.

'Wow,' I stuttered. 'You look ... ' I breathed out in a long whistle. 'You look amazing.'

He smiled broadly, showing his white, even teeth in one of the first real smiles I'd seen him give since we left Europe. 'This is my new uniform.' He spread his arms a little, glancing down at himself. 'Not a bad effort for a half-Italian, half-Montverrian. What do you think?'

'Not bad at all.' My face decided right then and there to turn a decided pink; and to hide the fact that I couldn't keep my eyes off him, I threw my arms around his neck and planted a kiss below his ear.

His arms encircled me, and he murmured, 'Ever made love to a man in a kilt?'

And after that, everything between us was perfect again. All my worries about

Léon wanting to go home to Italy and all his former tension vanished, and we were just as we had been during those idyllic two weeks we'd spent at his home on the Amalfi coast that summer.

But of course, perfect times can't last forever. Everything changed when I realised it wasn't Léon who was being followed.

It was me.

10

At first I didn't think anything of it. It started off in such a run-of-the-mill way. We'd run out of potatoes, and so I dropped in at my local greengrocer's on the way home to pick some up for our evening meal. I stepped inside the shop, letting the door shut behind me, and then remembered I'd forgotten to draw any money out from the cashpoint opposite. I turned and went straight back out, bumping slap bang into a skinny, hard-chested figure just outside the door.

'Ouch,' I said, rubbing my nose. A pair of startled blue eyes met mine for the briefest of seconds. I began to apologise for my clumsiness, but the young man turned abruptly and began to hurry off down the street, leaving a strong smell of cigarette smoke in his wake. He had dark, neatly cut hair and was wearing a black overcoat. He moved quickly, looking neither right nor left. I put his abruptness down to the fact he must have been in a rush, and I crossed over the road to the bank, thinking nothing of it.

But then the next day, as I was heading out of the rehearsal room chatting to Jeannie, the actress who was playing one of the witches, I saw the same man again. He was sitting at a table outside the café opposite, smoking a cigarette. He stood quickly and began to walk off. I sprang forward.

'What's the matter?' Jeannie cried, but I didn't answer. I was too intent on trying to get across the road. The traffic was heavy, and before I could even think of reaching the other side he'd got to a bus stop and boarded a bus. It pulled away, and he was gone.

A gap finally came in the steady stream of cars, and I decided to take a leaf out of Léon's book of sleuthing. I darted across the road and made my way to the table where the young man had been sitting. There was a partially smoked cigarette stubbed out in the ashtray. I held it to my nostrils and breathed in the sweet smell of French cigarettes.

'What on earth are you doing, Lizzie?'

I'd forgotten all about Jeannie. She'd crossed the road and was standing behind me, her expression a mixture of concern and fascination. I dropped the cigarette butt back in the ashtray and pulled out a tissue to wipe my hands. 'Have you ever seen that guy hanging around here before?' I asked. I nodded in the direction the young man had taken as he rushed off. And then Jeannie said something that only added to my suspicions.

'Aye, I have. He was outside the studio just a wee while back. Tuesday, maybe? Kind of a cute face close up. Cool overcoat. I asked if I could help, and he said, 'No, zank you ver-r-r-y much.'' Jeannie rolled the consonant in an excellent imitation and grinned widely. 'French accent and all. Is this another one of your admirers?'

That was no French accent she'd heard. The man had to be from Montverrier. I gazed back up the road in the direction the bus had taken, eyes narrowed. 'I thought I'd seen him before,' I said. 'And something about him gives me the creeps.'

Jeannie gave a disbelieving laugh. 'He can follow me any day of the week. He looks a honey.' She linked her arm through mine. 'You've been studying this damn Scottish play too long, that's what it is. Come on, let's get a cup of tea.'

I let myself be persuaded into the same café the Montverrian guy had just left. But despite Jeannie's cheerful gossip and the steaming brew, a sense of foreboding hung over me, and I had no idea what to do about it.

Back in the flat that evening, after we'd tidied away our dinner things and retired to the sitting-room, Léon drifted over to the window and began what had become an evening ritual of looking down on the Grassmarket. I moved to stand next to him and took a glance outside, but once again there was nothing to see but the usual groups strolling about in twos and threes.

'Have you seen him recently?' I asked.

Léon didn't blink. 'Seen who?' he replied coolly.

'Léon.' I tugged at his arm. 'I know you don't want to worry me, but you shouldn't keep secrets from me.'

And now all my worst fears were realised as his gaze held mine, hard and searching. 'What have you seen? And when?'

And so I explained about the man with the limp outside the greengrocer's who'd turned up a few days later outside the rehearsal studio. I mentioned how Jeannie had seen him, too, and about the way she'd mimicked his accent. And then I told him about the cigarette left in the ashtray.

'Do you think it could have been one of those same guys who were outside the restaurant the other night?' I tried to keep my voice steady, but the truth was, I was frightened.

Léon frowned down at the scene below. I didn't like seeing him at a loss, and my anxiety only increased. 'I don't know,' he said bluntly. 'I've met all the Montverrian guys in the team guarding the Scottish Diamond, and none of them have a limp. And none of them smoke. So it can't be any of them.'

'Then who … ?' The frown etched a black line in his brow. When he didn't answer straightaway, I said, 'Do you think we should go to the police?'

'No,' he said harshly. His eyes met mine swiftly, hard as ice. 'No police.'

I was taken aback. Léon must have registered my confusion because he dropped his gaze, but not before I'd caught a fleeting impression of the emptiness I'd thought had long gone. Then he turned his head, his profile stark against the yellow glow from the streetlights outside.

'There is no point involving the police,' he said, after a moment or two. 'What can we tell them? After all, what evidence do we have this man means any harm? And in any case, if there really is someone following you, I think he's an amateur. A dangerous man wouldn't have let himself be seen.'

His words did nothing to reassure me. I wrapped my arms around myself. Léon reached a hand up to caress my cheek, then let it fall to hang stiffly by his side. After a few seconds of silence, he said quietly, 'Perhaps it would be better if I returned to Italy.'

I jerked my head up. This was the last thing I'd expected him to say! I caught hold of his arm. 'Léon! Why?'

'I can't help thinking I'm only bringing you bad luck by being here. I've had to work too hard, trying to fit in. And now perhaps there's someone following you. None of this would have happened if I hadn't come here.'

I wrapped my arms around his waist, and strangely, I felt relief flood through me. All along I'd worried Léon might be regretting leaving Italy, when in fact it seemed he was worried he was making me unhappy. My voice was muffled in his chest. 'What's all the talk about bad luck? I'm the one who's supposed to be superstitious. And anyway, you're right. Even if I am being followed, my stalker doesn't look like he'd hurt a fly. Jeannie thinks he's cute.'

Léon threaded his hands through my hair. 'Even so, I mean to find out who he is. But in the meantime, you're not to take any chances. Whoever it is, from now on you're not to go anywhere alone.'

I drew back, gazing up at him in dismay. 'I go everywhere alone. And how on earth will I get to rehearsals? You can't come with me. You're already at work when I leave the house.'

'You must get a taxi every day to the rehearsal studio. Just until I've managed to find out who this man is, and what he's up to.'

I'd forgotten just how determined Léon could be at times. 'Fine,' I said reluctantly. 'But on one condition. No more talk of going back to Italy.' I met his gaze squarely. 'Is that a deal?'

There was the briefest of pauses before he replied, with a slow smile, 'It's a deal.'

11

When you discover you're being stalked in the streets of your home town by a stranger, it's reassuring to know you have a professional bodyguard at your back. And it's equally reassuring to find that your bodyguard has confidence in your ability to handle yourself. Léon treated me as an equal, teaching me how to take what precautions I could. I learned several ways to shake off a follower, and what to do in case of a sudden attack.

'There's no need for physical strength,' Léon told me when I looked doubtful. My stalker might be cute, as Jeannie described him, but I'd felt his hard chest that time I collided with him, and there was no doubt the odds would be against me if it came to a physical struggle.

'One way you can defend yourself is by screaming,' Léon said. 'It's a perfectly acceptable tactic. And a scream from a trained voice like yours will frighten him out of his wits.'

Léon was right. I'm used to projecting my voice on stage. I decided if anyone attacked me, I'd scream *'Fire!'* as loudly as I could. In the streets of Edinburgh, this should surely be enough to attract attention and scare an attacker away. If it didn't work, I'd keep my keys in my pocket at all times and be ready to stab him in the eye.

I found Léon's matter-of-fact approach reassuring. And after all, he reasoned, it was only during daylight hours that I would have to manage without him by my side. Besides, how far could my stalker go when I was surrounded by friends, in a crowded city, in daylight? And for the times when I needed to get somewhere by myself, I could call a cab from a trusted firm.

It was a nuisance having to take taxis everywhere, but since I'd promised Léon, I gave up my morning walk and began travelling to work by cab. The first day Jeannie discovered me paying off a taxi outside the rehearsal studio, she did a double-take.

'Travelling in style.' She nudged me with her elbow, with an amused glint in her eye. 'Did you sleep in? Or was Léon keeping you in bed?' She let out one of her giggles.

'Haha,' I replied. I turned my key in the lock of the studio door and pushed it open. 'Actually, Jeannie, I know this sounds weird, but it's that guy — the one we saw sitting outside the café the other day. I think he's following me.'

Jeannie regarded me as though I'd taken leave of my senses. 'That lovely guy with the dimples and the cool coat? You're not still fretting about him. Seriously?'

I swung the door shut behind us. Of course, I could see why Jeannie would find my anxiety incomprehensible. It was fantastical that anyone would want to follow me. But Jeannie didn't know Montverrier as I did. After spending the summer there with Léon, I'd discovered that it is a country shrouded in deceit. A fog of intrigue hangs like a pall over everything, and I'd been dogged by a constant feeling of foreboding ever since I'd first encountered the two Montverrians on the steps of Calton Hill and thought I'd heard them say Léon's name. And if Léon agreed I ought to take precautions, I definitely wasn't about to take any chances.

Jeannie followed me down the hallway into the rehearsal room. 'I still don't get it. I mean, has this guy actually done anything?'

We began to pull a few chairs into a semicircle, ready for our rehearsal. As we busied ourselves with getting the room ready, I told her, 'I know this sounds dramatic, Jeannie, but when I mentioned to Léon there was a guy hanging round here, he said it might be better if I didn't wander round Edinburgh on my own.'

Jeannie's face cleared as she pushed the final chair into position. 'Ah, that explains everything. Well, this is what comes of dating a bodyguard. I expect he sees danger everywhere. But honestly, this is Edinburgh — ' The front door opened and the cheerful voices of the other actors arriving cut short her reply.

I quickly laid my hand on Jeannie's arm. 'Listen, Jeannie. I know it sounds mad, but if anything does happen — I mean, if I don't turn up to rehearsals, or you think I've gone missing, you will call Léon straightaway and tell him?'

Jeannie patted my hand. 'Of course I will, hon. But I really think you're worrying over nothing. It's *Macbeth* I blame. This play's enough to give anyone the heebie jeebies.'

There was a collective intake of breath from the rest of the actors, who had now all entered the room and were staring at Jeannie, horrified. As silly as it sounds, my own heart plummeted into my boots as soon as she said the M-word, and I drew in a loud breath.

Jeannie clapped a hand to her mouth. 'Oops.' Her eyes brimmed with mortification. 'I'm so, so sorry!' She ran to the door and closed it behind her, and we caught the sound of her heels tapping the tiles in the hallway as she turned round

71

three times in rapid succession.

This was the second time the Scottish play's name had been uttered aloud in rehearsals. The rest of the actors and I all looked at each other. Although Léon would think me foolish for giving in to superstition, I gave a shiver of apprehension.

Jeannie came back in, flushed with embarrassment. The atmosphere in the room turned heavy and sullen, like the leaden mist around Shakespeare's witches.

12

When I told Léon about Jeannie's mistake during rehearsals, I was surprised to find that this time he didn't laugh off my superstition. He was quieter than usual, but I put this down to his concern about the fact that I was being followed.

I still often caught him standing with his arms crossed, gazing down into the street. Even when there was no further sign of my stalker as the days wore on, he continued to remain vigilant. To allay his anxiety, I would text him several times during the day to reassure him of my whereabouts.

After a week at his new job, Léon bought himself a motorbike, and every day he rode up the steep hill leading to the castle. After he'd gone, I'd climb into my taxi and make my way to rehearsals on the other side of town. A couple of weeks passed in this manner, and I caught no glimpse at all of my Montverrian follower — not even a whiff of cigarette smoke or a burnt-out stub on the pavement. We'd been rehearsing *Macbeth* solidly, and Jeannie's oversight in uttering its name out loud in rehearsals had so far brought us no ill luck whatsoever. In fact, rehearsals were going well, and I began to forget about Montverrier and look forward to our first performance.

One day Léon came home with an interesting story to tell me. Alexander Dalgliesh, the present Lord Falmire, had surprised everyone by turning up at the exhibition of the diamond. 'It was totally unexpected,' Léon said. 'The history of the diamond makes a fantastic story. If he'd told us he was coming, there would have been reporters all over the place, and even TV cameras, and he'd have had VIP treatment. But he played it all low-key. When he came into the exhibition room, though, I guessed immediately who he was from your description. The moustache gave him away,' he added with a grin. 'And then there's the fact that most people just admire the diamond for a short while and move on, but Lord Falmire stopped in front of the glass case and stared at it for a long time, circling round to examine it from every angle.

'I wasn't going to approach him — I thought he obviously wanted to be left alone — but he surprised me by introducing himself. Then he began chatting as though it was the most natural thing in the world to see his ancestor's diamond in an exhibition. He was a really pleasant man. When he heard my accent he asked if I was from Montverrier, and he switched to speaking French. He speaks it very well.'

'Really?' I couldn't help feeling surprised at this. I couldn't imagine this rather dour, quiet Scot chatting away to a stranger. 'He's not very talkative when he comes to our shows,' I told Léon. 'Quite the opposite.'

Léon turned a little pink in the cheeks. 'Yes, well,' he said. 'I think he took a shine to me.'

The penny dropped. 'Ooh, I see.' I

chuckled. 'Well, you do make a striking figure in that kilt.'

Léon grinned sheepishly. He seemed a little embarrassed to be teased, and so I took pity on him and changed the subject. 'So what did Lord Falmire talk about? Does he still maintain the diamond belongs to the Falmire family?'

Léon frowned a little. 'To be honest, he didn't talk much about the diamond. He asked me a lot about myself. Wanted to know where I'd worked in Montverrier, and to tell me how he'd often visited that country himself, and that was how he happened to speak such good French. He didn't appear to hold a grudge against the Montverrian royal family at all. On the contrary, he told me he hoped I was guarding the diamond well for the princess, and he asked me some questions about security. And at the end, just as he was going, he even mentioned you.'

'Me?' I turned round from the pan I was stirring and stared at Léon, astonished.

'Yes, you.' Léon smiled. 'He said he'd

heard your group was performing the Scottish play this year, and he looked forward to seeing it. He said you were a fine actress.'

The sauce in the pan was boiling, but I stood there nonplussed, with the wooden spoon in my hand. 'How on earth does he know about me?' I said. 'I mean, of course I've met him two or three times, but he doesn't know me at all. Not enough to know you're my boyfriend.'

Léon didn't seem to think it odd at all. 'He told me he'd been talking to Mr Ross recently, the director of your old drama college, and Mr Ross mentioned your plans to perform *Macbeth*. I guess they were bound to talk about the Scottish Diamond, too, given Falmire's connection, and that's how he discovered the coincidence that your boyfriend was part of security.'

I thought over Léon's words, my frown deepening. I suppose it seemed reasonable enough — the theatre world in Edinburgh is a small and gossipy one, and Mr Ross may very well have found out that I'd returned from Montverrier with Léon, and that Léon was working at the castle. Still, there was something odd about it.

Léon caught my expression. He came towards me, lifted a lock of my red hair, and began to curl it around his slender finger. 'As you said, everyone knows everyone in Edinburgh. And why wouldn't they talk about you?' He raised a hand to cup my cheek, studying my face. 'You're beautiful and talented and clever.'

He pulled me close and kissed me, and then I forgot everything that is, until the smell of the sauce beginning to burn in the pan made me break away and I had to rush to rescue it from the gas flame.

13

The superstitious jitters that had troubled my cast during rehearsals gradually lifted. In fact, *Macbeth* was shaping up to be one of the most gripping performances we had ever produced. The first time we had a full run-through, there was complete silence after Malcolm's final speech. Then someone started clapping, and we all broke into spontaneous applause. Jeannie had tears streaming down her face, and there was a lump in my own throat. We had put together a class performance.

I was still on a high after that full rehearsal as I waved goodbye to the other actors and climbed into my cab to go home. It had been a full two weeks since I'd last seen my neatly dressed stalker, and as I pulled on my seatbelt I decided to tell the taxi company I no longer needed their services. I missed my walks through Edinburgh, and if I was no longer being followed, taking a taxi every day was an unnecessary expense.

I clicked my belt into place and turned my head to the window ... and that's when I saw him. My stalker. He was leaning against the wall of the café on the other side of the road, a lit cigarette in one hand and a mobile phone pressed to his ear with the other. The taxi passed directly in front of him. His blue gaze met mine, and I caught a gleam of mockery. He continued to speak into his phone, lifting his chin and turning slightly to follow the direction of the taxi as it passed. I twisted right round in my seat to stare at him. Then the taxi rounded a corner, and he was gone.

I let out all the breath I'd kept in, my hands gripping the bag on my lap. The driver threw me a sideways glance. 'Aw richt, hen?'

I wondered whether to confess to this stranger that I thought I was being followed, and decided perhaps it was a good idea. If anything did happen, at least the taxi driver might remember me, and he'd be able to tell the police afterwards how I was convinced I had a stalker. A cold fear settled in the pit of my stomach. I opened my mouth to tell the driver my concerns, but just then the mobile phone in my bag gave a shrill ring. I leaped in my seat, astonishing the driver by letting out a startled cry, but I couldn't help it. To have my own phone go off when I'd just seen my stalker with a mobile in his hand ... !

I drew the phone out and checked the screen. Private number. Could it be him? I contemplated ignoring it for a second, but that's all it was — just a fleeting instant of cowardice. I was determined not to be bullied. I straightened myself in my seat and pressed the button to accept the call.

'Hello?' I was glad to note my voice was calm, with none of the shakiness evident in my hands.

'Am I speaking to Elizabeth Smith?' The voice at the other end of the phone was soft and courteous, with a cultured Scottish accent. No trace of Montverrian at all. I sank back in my seat, almost sighing out loud with relief.

'Speaking.'

'Hello, Elizabeth. This is Alexander Dalgliesh here.'

In an instant I was upright again, jaw open. Lord Falmire! The real owner of the Scottish Diamond. What sort of a coincidence was this?

'Hello?' he said again. 'Elizabeth? Are you still there?'

'Yes. Yes, I'm still here. How can I help?'

'I was given your number by Charles Ross at your old drama college. As you know, I'm heavily involved in promoting the arts in Midlothian, and Charles tells me your theatre is rehearsing the Scottish play. There's something I'd like to discuss with you about a possible performance.'

The furious pounding of my heart began to slow. Not such a coincidence to hear from Lord Falmire — after all, as Léon had already said, he'd been speaking to Mr Ross. And my ears pricked up at the mention of a possible extra performance. If Lord Falmire was offering us the chance of putting on a show, or even a run of shows, then that was great news for the cast, and we were always in need of money and publicity.

I put my business voice on. 'Do you have a particular date in mind? And an audience?'

'Aye. It's only a wee theatre, but it would definitely be worth your while. Perhaps you'd like to discuss it. Would you have time this evening, say?'

I thought of my stalker again. I was desperate to see Léon and tell him all about it, and the last thing I wanted was to leave my flat that evening. There was nothing I'd have loved better than to refuse, but I was conscious of the rest of my acting team and how important this might be to them.

As though guessing my dilemma, Alexander Dalgliesh added, 'It's an interesting proposition I have, and I think you'll find it's to our mutual benefit.'

'Thank you,' I said, hiding my reluctance. 'I'd be delighted to meet up.'

'Good. I'll come and pick you up in half an hour.' I opened my mouth to protest that this wouldn't give me nearly enough time to gather myself, but he added quickly, 'I look forward to seeing you,' and then the phone went dead.

I gazed at its blank screen, both puzzled and astonished. But we were drawing near my flat, and so I had no time to ponder on Lord Falmire's call. It was a nuisance, as now I'd have no time to tell Léon about my stalker. He wasn't due home from his job at the castle for another hour or so, by which time I'd be at my meeting with Lord Falmire. Still, it couldn't be helped. I'd just have to leave Léon a note, and tell him about the mysterious Montverrian when I got home again.

I paid off the taxi driver, and it wasn't until I was mounting the steps to my flat and had the key in the door that I remembered I hadn't even given Lord Falmire my address, and yet he'd offered to pick me up. How did he know where I lived? It was most unlike Mr Ross to give out personal details. I pushed the door open, feeling annoyed.

14

I swept into the hall, dumping my bag on the side table, and rushed upstairs to get changed out of the leggings I'd been rehearsing in. I only just had time to brush my hair and pull on a smart top and grey pleated skirt before the doorbell rang. I glanced at my watch. Only a quarter of an hour had passed since Lord Falmire's call. I flew downstairs, and when I opened the door a little breathlessly there he was on the doorstep, looking sheepish.

'I'm a little early,' he said, shuffling his feet with that hint of polite Scots embarrassment at causing another person inconvenience. 'I'm sorry to rush you, but I have another appointment this evening.'

'No problem,' I said smoothly, although obviously of course it was. I was breathless and had hardly had time to gather my thoughts. Inwardly I shook my head at my response. Honestly, why were we Scots always so crippled by courtesy?

Lord Falmire towered in the doorway, smoothing down his reddish moustache in a nervous gesture. I'd forgotten how large he was. He was neatly dressed in dark trousers and a navy blazer-style jacket, looking exactly as though he were on his way to a meeting of the golf club.

'I'll just get my bag,' I told him, stepping back into the hall. 'And I need to leave a note for my boyfriend.'

'No need for that.' His tone was so sharp I turned back in astonishment. His unnerving gaze met mine, but he gave me another embarrassed smile, rocking on his heels. 'I'm sorry,' he said.

By this time I'd lost count of the number of times he'd apologised. He gestured over his shoulder, and I made out a maroon-coloured Jaguar double-parked on the busy street at the bottom of the steep steps to my flat.

'My driver's waiting. Would it be possible to send your boyfriend a text when we're on our way?' His tone was perfectly pleasant, but I thought Lord Falmire was becoming a little high-handed. Perhaps the aristocracy were used to having every whim met. Still, it was a reasonable enough request.

I picked up my bag from the side-table and lifted my coat off the hook. He stood back courteously, allowing me to lead the way down the stone steps and onto the pavement. I could see his need for hurry. The Jaguar's engine was running, and his driver was clutching the wheel, obviously anxious to be off, his head turned towards the busy road. Falmire opened the rear passenger door for me and I climbed inside. Then he completely took me aback by getting in on the same side as I did, edging me up the seat with his large frame and forcing me to scramble inelegantly along to the other side, so that I was sitting behind the driver. He pulled the door shut and settled back to look at me. I must have shown my mingled astonishment and annoyance, as his expression was nervous, and there were two white lines either side of his nostrils. This time he didn't apologise again.

The car set off with a jerk I wasn't prepared for, and my head fell back against the leather upholstery. I had to hold myself steady by grabbing hold of the driver's seat in front of me. Lord Falmire, too, seemed thrown by the speed of our departure. '*Attention, Raymond!*' he told the driver sharply. '*On veut pas se faire arrêté, quand même!*'

'*T'inquiète pas.*' I speak fluent French. It's the official language of Montverrier, and after my summer there my brain was still in tune with it. I understood Falmire's tart command to the driver to pay attention, since they didn't 'want to get arrested, for goodness's sake'. I was tired after rehearsals, though, and it took me a full second to register that it wasn't usual for a Scottish person to speak French to his driver, or for the driver to answer so pertly with the informal '*tu*'.

And Lord Falmire had called him Raymond. The name rang a bell from somewhere ... I tilted my head a little in order to catch a glimpse of the driver in his rear-view mirror. A pair of mocking blue eyes met mine, and suddenly everything in my brain was a completely terrified blank. Looking back at me in the rectangle of glass above the windscreen was my stalker. He gave me a grin, and one of his blue eyes closed in a wink before he returned his attention to the road.

I pressed back rigid on the seat. For one terrified second there was utter silence. And then I drew in my breath. '*Fi-i-i-ire!*' I screamed.

'For the love of God!' Falmire reached across and clamped his broad hand tightly around my mouth. 'Shut up, woman.' He pulled me to him with a surprising amount of strength and wrapped his other arm around my stomach, gripping me tightly. I'd become twisted in my seat, and now my back was towards him and I was wedged uncomfortably against his slightly squashy chest, facing the door.

Raymond continued on his way, humming a little under his breath. Outside the window the streets were full of people walking by purposefully. It was commuter hour, and the city workers were hurrying home. We passed a bus stop full of office workers in suits and dark skirts. It seemed to me impossible that not one of these people had heard me shout out, since my scream could have lifted the roof off Holyrood Palace. My eyes roved the street frantically, but it was useless. Every single person we passed either had their attention glued to the screen on their phone or else was focused on the sounds coming from the headphones clamped to their heads. All were entirely oblivious to what was happening to me.

What has this city come to? I thought desperately. *Is everyone so tuned out of their surroundings that they can't see or hear what's around them?*

Lord Falmire's hand gripped my mouth painfully. I tried to open my lips to bite him, but his strong fingers were under my jaw, clamping it shut. I wriggled furiously and managed to raise one leg, which I began to thump hard against the door. A little boy holding his father's hand heard me as we passed, and I felt a flicker of hope when the child began tugging on his dad's sleeve, pointing in my direction. But my hope was short-lived. The father frowned down at his son and carried on talking into his mobile. A second later, they'd slid out of view.

I redoubled my effort to wrest myself free of Lord Falmire. 'Elizabeth, will you please stop struggling?' His voice lost its smooth civility to become distinctly edgy. 'We have a long drive to Helstone House and I don't want to arrive exhausted.'

Helstone House! Lord Falmire's stately pile was a good half an hour out of Edinburgh, and set back in large grounds. If they were taking me there, what on earth were they planning to do? I began twisting like a salmon on the end of a line, banging my foot on the door as hard as I could, trying to stop the terror welling in my gorge. I thought I might throw up, and my nausea wasn't helped when Falmire pushed his bulky frame forward so that I was pinned to the seat, doubled over with my face near my own thighs, hardly able to breathe.

'Please calm down,' he said. 'All we

want to do is have a quiet talk about your boyfriend.'

I stiffened, my mind racing. What did he know about Léon? Was he after the diamond? And how much did they know about my stay in Montverrier? Lord Falmire's next words made my blood freeze.

'Any more trouble from you, and Raymond here will make a phone call to some of his Montverrian friends. And — how shall I put this? Raymond's Montverrian friends aren't quite as, er, shall we say *civilised* as I am, and if you refuse to co-operate it will be the worse for your good-looking bodyguard. To put it bluntly, he might lose some of his looks. Do I make myself clear, Elizabeth?'

There was a momentary tightening of his arm around my waist. I fell perfectly still. My heart hammered in my chest, and apart from its thudding and the sound of Lord Falmire's quick breathing, there was silence for several seconds. Slowly, Falmire removed his hand from my mouth and moved back to his own side of the car. I raised myself, righted my skirt, and sat with my hands loosely folded in my lap, gazing forward, my expression rigid, swallowing the bile in my throat.

Who were Raymond's Montverrian friends? The two men who'd passed by that day on Calton Hill? The whole group of them who'd been talking so loudly in the courtyard of Edinburgh castle? Or was it all a bluff to scare me, and Raymond was acting alone? I tried to slow the maelstrom of my thoughts as I turned over the possibilities. Then I thought of Léon, and my heart banged hard in my chest. I had to remain calm. His safety could depend on it.

'There.' Falmire smoothed his trousers and tugged at the lapels of his blazer. 'Isn't this much more civilised?'

I clamped my lips together on a venomous reply. I'd once heard that if ever you're interrogated, you should say as little as possible. Of course I hadn't ever thought that day would arise for me, but I decided complete silence was my best policy. Plus I needed time to think, and my mind was alive with conjecture. What on earth did Falmire want from us? It must surely have something to do with the Scottish diamond. My fear mounted at the realisation they were probably kidnapping me in order to lure Léon into danger. I forced myself to take a few deep breaths. *Think!*

Then I remembered my mobile phone, which was in the bag at my feet. Of course! I raised my head a little and found Raymond looking at me in his mirror again through narrowed eyes. I stared back, using every atom of my acting training to keep my expression neutral.

15

For several minutes none of us said a word. Raymond turned his gaze back to the road. The car was now heading away west out of the city. Beside me, Falmire rested his hands on his knees and leaned back in his seat. I took the opportunity to slip my feet out of my shoes as surreptitiously as I could. I nudged my bag with my toes, feeling for the clasp. If I could just edge the bag open, I might be able to get a foot inside and draw out my phone.

I was concentrating so hard on my task that I nearly jumped in my seat when Raymond flicked on the radio and pop music began to blare out through the expensive sound system right behind my head. I waited for Falmire to tell him to turn it down, and was astonished when instead he began tapping his knee in time to the music. I recognised the song, which had won the Eurovision song contest a few years previously. The jaunty tune filled the car, giving me a sense of the surreal.

I redoubled my efforts to retrieve my mobile. Luckily I'd brought my vintage handbag with me — the one with the worn clasp. It took only a slight pressure with my big toe to work it open. I took another glance in the mirror before swivelling my gaze sideways to where Falmire was sitting. Despite the pounding of my heart I sat perfectly still, my hands resting loosely in my lap, for all the world as though we were just a group of pop lovers on a pleasant outing to the outskirts of Edinburgh.

I wriggled one stockinged foot into the interior of my bag and thanked the few lucky stars that were left shining over me that the sound of Europop blaring from the speakers drowned out the rustling I was making. I poked around, lifting my purse gingerly with my toes until — there it was! I carefully slid out the slim rectangle that was my phone until it was lying in the footwell. Now what? I forced my chest to rise and then to fall slowly on a quiet outbreath. Then I ducked down quickly.

'Where's my shoe?' I said, my voice muffled as I fumbled on the floor. I picked up my mobile and slid it swiftly up the sleeve of my blouse. 'Ah, there it is.' I pushed my foot back inside the shoe I'd kicked off earlier and righted myself with a smile.

Lord Falmire eyed me suspiciously. The track on the radio changed, and I recognised a group who were now more middle-aged men than the boy band the DJ introduced them as. I tilted my head to one side as though listening. Falmire eyed me with that unsettling expression he had. He knew I was playing at something, but couldn't fathom what. I returned his gaze, and for a couple of seconds we stared each other out.

And then, with a shrill, insistent ring that was far louder than the radio, the mobile in my sleeve burst into life, startling both of us and causing my heart to leap in my ribcage.

16

Lord Falmire and I both moved as one, but I was quicker. I shot out my phone in an instant and bent double so that my head was deep in the footwell, and the phone beyond Falmire's grasp. 'Léon!' My voice was strangled and I tried to breathe in, but I could hardly raise my chest, doubled over as I was. 'I've been abducted by Lord Falmire and he's taking me to — '

Falmire threw himself on my back, grappling with my arm. The phone fell from my hand with a thud. The screen's light shone back at me from the expensive carpet on the floor, and I heard Léon's voice say faintly, and with his usual calm, 'Lizzie? Where are you?'

It was such a relief to hear him safe and well that I almost sobbed aloud. Falmire was gripping me tightly. The phone had fallen out of my reach, but

I managed to shout out that I was OK before my ribcage was crushed into my knees. I watched helplessly as Falmire's hand reached down beside me to grope around until his fingers found my phone. He picked it up and righted himself.

'Léon,' he said into the handset, his smooth voice only slightly breathless. 'I'm so glad you called. I would have phoned you myself when we arrived at Helstone. I'm sorry you had to hear the news in such a dramatic way, but you know actors.' He caught my eye with a sarcastic smile. 'Always ready with the melodrama.'

I lunged for the phone, calling Léon's name again, but Falmire held up a hand and pushed me back forcefully. He dropped the phone from his ear. 'Elizabeth, if you give me any more trouble, Raymond will be forced to phone his Montverrian friends and ask them to pay Léon a visit.' His eyes pierced mine, as hard as the Scottish Diamond. 'And I'm sure you wouldn't want that.'

Once more I thought of the group of

dark-suited men I'd seen with Léon in the courtyard at Edinburgh Castle. Were those men really in league with Lord Falmire? It didn't make sense. I glanced at Raymond's reflection in the rear-view mirror. What was a Montverrian doing driving Falmire's car? I couldn't understand any of it. Raymond's eyes met mine briefly, and he shrugged sympathetically, as though matters were out of his power. Then he returned his gaze to the road ahead, leading away from Edinburgh.

Everywhere I looked, there was shifting sand. It was as though my rehearsals for *Macbeth* had followed me into real life, and I was surrounded by a fog of mischief and intrigue. I shook my head, trying to dispel the mist from my vision.

Falmire took the gesture for submission. He gave me a grim nod and returned to the phone. 'Apologies for the interruption, Léon —' I heard Léon's voice break in, but couldn't make out what he'd said. Falmire gave a dry laugh. 'Yes, you heard correctly. I'm taking Elizabeth to Helstone. And I have a proposal for you. A bargain, so to speak.' He tutted, clearing his throat. 'How I do hate a vulgar trade, but needs must.'

There was complete silence at the other end of the phone. I knew Léon well enough by now to know that he wouldn't waste his breath on unnecessary speech. He would be completely focused on listening intently to the background noise and for any more word from me. 'I'm all right!' I shouted as loudly as I could. I thought Léon might be able to use any information I could give him, and so I blurted out hurriedly, 'We're in Falmire's car. It's a maroon Jag. My stalker is driving. His name is Raymond. We've just passed — '

Falmire covered the phone and gave me a pained look. 'Elizabeth, could you please stop shouting.' He returned to Léon. 'As you can no doubt hear, Elizabeth is quite well.' He gave me a sidelong glance and added, with a mixture of apology and threat, 'For the moment. If you'd like to make your way to Helstone House, you can take her home. Unharmed.' He let out a sigh. 'And now the tedious question of a trade. All you need do in order to collect Elizabeth safe and sound is bring me the Scottish Diamond. The one that is rightfully mine.'

For a second I was too stunned to speak. Then I drew in my breath with a loud gasp and shouted out, 'That's stealing. Don't do it, Léon!'

'It's not stealing,' Falmire said harshly. 'The diamond belongs to me. It was stolen from my family by those plebeian upstarts in Montverrier.'

No reply came from the other end of the phone. I held my breath. Falmire and I both listened, the seconds ticking by. It seemed an eternity before Léon's voice came again. I strained to hear what he was saying, but could make out nothing except that he spoke slowly and with complete calm.

Falmire listened intently. 'Very good,' he said. 'We'll see you soon. And of course I needn't tell a bright young man like you to come alone. Elizabeth's safety depends on it.'

He ended the call and held my phone out as though to return it to me, but when I tried to take it he whisked it away, slipping it into the breast pocket of his blazer with a satisfied smile. 'What an enterprising young man your boyfriend is. I knew as soon as I met him that I could rely on him to arrange everything. He'll arrive at Helstone tonight. And he'll be bringing the diamond with him.'

He leaned back in his seat, eyes gleaming triumph. In front of me Raymond made some comment in French about my boyfriend being cute. I caught his eye and he raised an eyebrow, giving me an ironic smile. I noted a glance flash between Raymond and Lord Falmire. The thought struck me that Raymond wasn't Falmire's driver at all — he was his boyfriend. That would explain his use of the informal '*tu*'.

And then out of nowhere I remembered where I'd heard the name Raymond before. Of course! The missing security guard from the castle. The one those men from Montverrier had been talking about in the courtyard, that day they offered Léon work. A couple more pieces in the jigsaw slotted into place, but the whirling in my brain failed to slow down. I needed to find a way to escape and get back to Léon before he did anything reckless — like stealing the Princess of Montverrier's priceless jewel in order to rescue me.

I turned to the window. We had left the city streets and were racing down a dual carriageway. Even if I could have opened the door — which Raymond had surely locked, in any case — leaping out just here would mean serious injury or death. My phone was in Lord Falmire's pocket, and I'd already had a taste of the man's physical strength. Wresting my mobile back to phone for help wasn't an option.

Raymond reached forward to fiddle with the heater on the dashboard and we lost a little speed. It was now or never, and I'd have to seize my chance. As soon as Raymond leaned back, I was ready. I rose from my seat to throw my hands over his eyes, and I squeezed them shut, as hard as I possibly could.

17

The car lurched hideously.

'What the bloody hell do you think you're doing?' For the first time, Falmire lost his well-bred cool and gave a horrified shout. The car swerved dangerously near the barrier between the other carriageway and us.

'*Putain!* Get her off me!' Raymond cried out.

I squeezed harder, pressing with all my might. Raymond took his foot off the accelerator and began to brake, twisting his head from side to side. There came a blaring of horns behind us, and a car shot past, overtaking us in the slow lane.

'For God's sake!' Falmire gripped hold of my nearest wrist and wrenched it back with iron strength, twisting my arm so painfully I was forced to release Raymond at once. I fell back with a cry. 'Do you want to get us all killed?'

'Keep that bitch under control!' Raymond shouted.

'I am not a — '

Falmire silenced my next words by grabbing hold of my mouth with his strong hand and dragging me down on the seat. I struggled with all the strength I possessed, but he raised himself from his seat and sat back down again on my chest, forcing the wind out of me. He was breathing heavily.

'Now, I was hoping we could proceed in a civilised fashion,' he said, beginning to take off his tie, 'but you've given me no other option.' He was weighting my chest and arms down, but my legs were free, and I began kicking against the door again, screaming as loudly as I could. He stopped what he was doing with his tie and fished out a silk handkerchief from his pocket, which he proceeded to force into my mouth mid-scream. I caught the overpowering scent of expensive cologne and almost gagged.

While I struggled with the handkerchief, trying to spit it out, Falmire caught hold of my wrists and began to bind them together with his tie. He pulled the silk tight in a painful knot, and after a few minutes' frantic struggling I eventually found myself lying flat on my back, with Falmire now sitting on my legs instead of my chest. My hands were bound, and he managed to raise my arms above my head and secure my wrists to the door handle with one end of his tie, so now I couldn't move at all. I lay there panting through my nose while Falmire made a show of brushing down his jacket. There were a couple of drops of sweat on his brow. He lifted a hand to the bridge of his nose and squeezed it, shutting his eyes and taking deep, slow breaths.

For a while, no one said anything. I couldn't speak, in any case, trussed up as I was with Lord Falmire's silk handkerchief still rammed in my mouth. Then I heard Raymond say in a long-suffering voice, 'I told you this wouldn't be easy.'

'Shut up,' Falmire replied. He leaned his head back on the seat, where he remained with his eyes closed.

I turned my head to one side and finally managed to dislodge the handkerchief. For the rest of the journey, none of us said a word.

18

During that silence, while Falmire sat there with his eyes shut and Raymond concentrated on the road ahead, all sorts of things went through my mind, but one thought stood out like a burning torch lighting the way through a Scottish mist. You might find this strange perhaps, but my overriding memory from the terror of that journey is that I finally realised just how desperately in love I was with Léon. I was gagged and bound, alone in a car with a maniac and his sidekick, and yet all I could worry about was what Léon was doing. Was he really going to steal the Scottish Diamond? What would happen if he got caught? And would Falmire just let him go home after he'd handed it over? I was consumed with fear for him.

It grew darker and darker. Night had fallen, and we had long since left the suburbs of Edinburgh. Eventually there were no streetlights at all, just great black trees overhanging the road. Lord Falmire and I were both tightly wound with tension — a state that obviously didn't affect Raymond, who hummed along to the radio.

Finally we slowed to a halt. Raymond's window descended smoothly and he reached out to press a button on a post beside the road. I couldn't see much, lying bound as I was, but I heard a click and the sound of gates opening. And then we were through and into the grounds of Helstone House. As the gates swung shut behind us, the tension ebbed away from Lord Falmire.

'Home at last,' he said. 'And please don't scream as we draw up. It's very wearing on my ears, and completely pointless. No one can hear you.'

He leaned over and tugged at the knots he'd made in his tie. A scowl darkened his smooth features. 'That's ruined a perfectly good tie.' Eventually he managed to work me free.

I sat up, rubbing my wrists, to find

that we were on a long, narrow drive approaching the grand façade of the house. A yellow light spilled out from one or two of the windows, but apart from that, the entire place was in darkness, and I guessed we were alone. I wondered how on earth Léon would manage to find his way. Then we were rounding the front of the house, and Raymond pulled up beside a set of steps leading down towards a basement. I was obviously being bundled in through the servants' entrance.

Raymond got out and opened Falmire's door first, and then they both came round to my side of the car. A blast of cold, damp air hit me as my door opened. 'Welcome to Helstone,' Raymond intoned, holding out a hand, an ironic smile on his face.

He and Falmire each took tight hold of one of my arms — although where they thought I could run to, I don't know. The next minute I was being marched down the steps and straight into a long, pristine kitchen with fashionable bare brick walls and the remains of a fire smouldering in a range. My first impression was one of fastidious neatness.

Falmire locked the door behind him and leaned back against it. 'Can I offer you a cup of tea?' he asked. 'Darjeeling? Earl Grey? Builder's?' Raymond made his way to one of the worktops and switched on a kettle. 'And I daresay you haven't eaten,' Falmire carried on, his voice full of solicitude. He bustled over to a large fridge in one corner, and while Raymond organised the tea things, he began pulling out a quiche, a glass bowl full of salad, and a plateful of ham. 'Please,' he said, gesturing to the oak table in the middle of the room, 'take a seat.'

There was a clock on the wall — one of those trendy minimalist ones with just two brass hands and no numbers. Still not even seven o'clock. I wondered when Léon would arrive. I'd given up all thought of escape, as during the last few minutes of the journey I'd decided it would be better now to wait here for Léon rather than to rush off into the grounds and risk us missing each other altogether. And then I saw the security monitor perched discreetly on one of the worktops, waiting to flicker into life should anyone be found in the grounds. Even if I did manage to escape, I'd never be able to find my way back to the gate unseen.

I went to the table, pulled out a chair and sat down, as instructed. I thought of my phone, which was still in Falmire's possession. If I could only wrest it back … At that very moment it rang again, loud and shrill, from his blazer pocket. The sound startled us both, and I leaped out of my chair. Falmire dropped the cutlery he was carrying, the knives and forks bouncing on the stone floor with a clatter.

'Hell and damnation!' He reached into his pocket, rolling his eyes when he saw the name flashing on the screen. He shoved the phone back, and it continued to give out a muffled ring.

'Who is it?' I asked.

'Only Jeannie. Whoever she is.' He knelt to pick up the fallen cutlery.

'She's my friend,' I protested. 'It might be important.'

Falmire stood, brushing the dust off his knees with a frown. 'Of course it isn't important.'

The phone stopped ringing abruptly. How I would have loved to have been at home in my cosy flat, listening to Jeannie's cheerful voice inviting me out to a bar in the old town. I had never felt more alone.

19

By now I was very, very afraid — but not for myself. My fear was all for Léon. I hid my terror under a mask of civility, joining in Lord Falmire's pretence that I was here purely by invitation. Falmire played the part of genial host so well, I half-wondered if he were more than a little unhinged, and had actually forgotten I was here by force. Now that he had me inside Helstone House, he was surprisingly relaxed and sure of himself.

Once he'd finished fussing over arranging our supper things, we all sat down at the table like a mismatched set of dinner-party guests. Falmire kept up an easy flow of small talk with Raymond, trying now and again to draw me into the conversation, for all the world as though I were just a shy guest in need of encouraging.

Every time I thought of Léon alone in

the Museum Room at Edinburgh Castle, removing the Scottish Diamond from the glass case, my mouth went dry. I pushed the food around on my plate, uneaten.

After what seemed like hours, I glanced at the clock on the wall. Its hands had barely moved. The waiting was intolerable, and in the end I could stand it no longer. I slammed my hand down on the table, making Falmire leap in his seat and the supper things rattle. 'How on earth do you think you're going to get away with this?'

Falmire broke off his conversation and turned to me with a look of pained surprise. 'Elizabeth —'

'Do you seriously think Léon is going to walk in here and hand over a priceless diamond? Just like that?'

Falmire opened his mouth, but I rushed on, answering for him. 'Of course he isn't. It's madness! And even if he did, as soon as the people at the castle discover the jewel is missing, they'll be straight onto us all. You'll never get away with it!'

'Ah,' Falmire said, putting a hand to his brow. 'Of course, how silly of me. Raymond, do you mind — ?'

Raymond put down his cutlery and rose from the table with a long-suffering look. From a drawer in the kitchen he drew out a small plastic box. He returned to the table and placed it in front of me.

'What's this?'

Raymond returned to his meal. Falmire continued to look at me with a small, satisfied smile. 'Take a look inside.'

I lifted the lid and my hand froze in mid-air. There, lying loose on a bed of ordinary cotton wool, was the most beautiful jewel I'd ever seen — a glittering teardrop, tinged with blue. I remembered Léon's vivid description: *as though wept from the eye of a goddess'*. The diamond caught the light from the kitchen, giving a soft sparkle. I stared at it in amazement. The Scottish Diamond! The very same priceless jewel Falmire had asked Léon to steal. I raised my head, my eyes swimming. What on earth did it all mean?

'Astonishing, isn't it?' Falmire said.

'This, my dear Elizabeth, is a perfect replica of the Scottish Diamond. Legend has it that when my ancestor fled to Montverrier — where he was so treacherously murdered — he left the replica behind in his wife's keeping. It's been in the family for generations. We children used to play with it. In fact, my housekeeper found it lying forgotten inside a doll's house as we were clearing out the old nursery. She polished off the dust and the grubby finger marks, and you can see for yourself it looks good as new.'

I drew out the fake diamond, letting it rest on my palm. The replica was cold and surprisingly heavy. When I moved it, a gentle light danced and sparkled over its surface.

'A thing of rare beauty,' Falmire said. 'And impossible to distinguish from the original with the naked eye. This is how I propose to 'get away with it', to use your vulgar phrase. When your young man brings us the real diamond, we'll give him this in its place. Léon will return to the castle with the replica this evening, place it in the case, and tomorrow no one will be any the wiser.'

I sat there, speechless. Of all the ways Falmire could have answered my question, I would never have expected this. The replica jewel sparkled in my palm, a splendid thing. If this was just a fake, I began to understand why Falmire coveted the original so much. Some of my fear began to abate. Was it really possible Léon could substitute the fake diamond without anyone knowing?

But then I came to my senses. Of course Falmire couldn't be allowed to get away with it. As soon as we got out of Helstone House, we would have to go straight to the police. I returned the fake jewel to its nest of cheap cotton wool. I couldn't believe that Falmire hadn't considered the possibility that we would go straight to the law. When I looked up, he was examining me with a quizzical look, and I found I was right. He guessed immediately what I was thinking.

His voice was all geniality. 'So,' he said, 'now you understand how with Léon's assistance it's perfectly possible to get away with the theft. And of course, neither of you will want to go to the police.'

I said nothing. Since we certainly would want to go to the police, there was no reply I could give.

'I see you don't believe me.' He chuckled. 'Perhaps I can persuade you how foolish you would be. First of all, there's the little matter of your deception in Montverrier this summer. If you so much as whisper a word to the police, we intend to reveal the truth. When the press find out that it was Elizabeth Smith from Edinburgh who was crowned in the cathedral — and not, in fact, Princess Charlotte of Montverrier — they'll have a field day. Quite the dramatic secret, isn't it? A story that will run and run for months. And since you swore an oath of secrecy, I'm sure you won't want it to come to light, especially as the scandal will bring down the Montverrian monarchy.'

I thought of the way the Princess of Montverrier had deceived me that summer; how she'd used me as a decoy, and how I'd been shot at by protesters during the ceremony. I remembered, too, how if it hadn't been for Léon, I could have died during the procession back from the Cathedral.

I gave a cold shrug. 'I've kept my oath. It's not my fault if someone else discovers the truth, so go to the press if you want to. Do your worst. Quite frankly, I don't give a damn.'

Lord Falmire gave a flinch of pain. 'Dear me.' He gave me a mournful look. 'Where is your loyalty to the aristocracy? You young people and your liberal ways. The next thing we know, there'll be revolution in the streets.'

I narrowed my eyes, thinking again of the princess's duplicity, and now Lord Falmire's lunatic abduction of me. They were neither of them great advertisements for an inherited title. 'A revolution?' I said. 'Bring it on.'

Falmire shook his head in despair. 'What an unreliable rabble you actors are.' And then, unbelievably, his voice became tinged with regret, and he genuinely seemed quite sad. 'I had hoped an appeal to your loyalty to the Montverrian royal family might be enough.' I gave an inelegant snort. Falmire carried on. 'Since you've closed that avenue to me, you've left me no option but to use my last resort.'

By now, although I knew perfectly well that Falmire meant business regarding stealing the diamond, I was no longer afraid for my physical safety. He seemed far too fastidious to offer real violence. I gazed around the kitchen and the remains of our genteel supper lying on the table. 'What are you going to do?' I asked him. 'Silence me with a butter knife?'

It was then that Raymond spoke to me directly for the first time since we'd sat down to our meal. He put down his fork and reached inside his jacket. 'No,' he said calmly. 'We'll kill you with this.' He pointed a gun at my chest and I drew back with a start, my chair legs scraping the stone floor with a teeth-jarring screech.

'For God's sake!' I cried out. 'Are you insane?'

Falmire let out a disappointed sigh. 'Raymond, Raymond. You're frightening the lassie. Please,' he told me, 'accept my apologies. Raymond here isn't used to our Scottish manners. We've no intention of killing either you or that handsome young man of yours. Raymond, put the gun away.'

Raymond put the gun back inside his jacket with a shrug. 'It was just a joke.'

The fear that had left me as I listened to Lord Falmire's inane small talk over supper returned with double the force. My hands trembled as I rested them back on the table. 'Is that thing loaded?' I asked. When Raymond merely gave me an ironic glance, I burst out, 'What the hell do you think you're playing at, carrying a loaded gun at the dinner table? If that's your idea of a joke, it's not funny!'

'Aye,' echoed Falmire. 'The lassie's right. Take the gun away, Raymond, and put it in one of the drawers.'

Raymond dropped his napkin on his

plate and stood. I didn't take my eyes off him as he crossed the room. He put his hand in his jacket to retrieve the gun but, instead of putting it safely away in a drawer, he laid it on the kitchen counter. He returned to his meal as calmly as if he'd just been asked to put down the book he'd been reading.

'That's much better,' Falmire said, casting a final glare at Raymond. 'Nobody here is going to get shot. I abhor violence.' He gave a fastidious shudder, glancing round at his pristine kitchen. 'And I won't have blood spilled in my house.'

Then he placed his elbows on the table and fixed me with his unnerving gaze. 'It pains me to have to do this, Elizabeth, but you see, it's like this. Once Léon has arrived and handed over the diamond as arranged, you will both leave freely.' He gave a wave towards the door. 'And neither of you will go to the police.'

I scowled. 'I don't believe you. You know we'd go straight to the police. As soon as we walk out of that door, Raymond will be after us with his gun, shooting us in the back and burying us in the grounds.' My voice rose on the last words and I tried desperately to control myself.

'Raymond won't do anything of the sort,' Falmire said in the tones one would use to placate a small child. 'You see, if you do go to the police, I'll tell them the whole thing was entirely Léon's idea. I'll tell them he offered to steal the diamond for me in return for payment. And since your young man already has a criminal record and has spent time in prison, and I am a peer of the realm without so much as a speeding ticket, which one of us do you think they're likely to believe?'

It took several seconds before Falmire's meaning sank in. Léon, a convicted criminal? It wasn't possible. I stared at Falmire, searching his face for signs he was lying, but there was a look of pity in his eyes that convinced me more than anything else would have done. With a sickening feeling, I realised just how very little I knew of Léon's past. He'd done his national service with the Montverrian army, he'd spent time in Switzerland and Italy, but what else did I really know?

The look of pity on Falmire's face intensified, and he shook his head. 'Dear, dear. I genuinely hate to be the one to spoil love's young dream, but I see it's as I thought. He hasn't told you anything of his criminal past, has he?'

He rose from the table and made his way to the counter, where a silver tablet was charging next to a socket. He came back, flipping through the screens. 'Here we are.' He held the tablet in front of me. 'Perhaps now you'll believe me.'

The headline was in Italian. I can speak a very little of the language. Enough to know that a young man named Léon Solara had been sentenced to prison for two years for his part in a robbery. There was no photo — just a picture of a freight train, which had come to a halt in the Italian countryside. Relief flooded through me. I glanced up at Falmire.

'You've made a mistake. Léon's name isn't Solara. It's Bressac. Léon Bressac.'

Falmire picked up the tablet and

scrolled down the screen before pushing it back towards me. 'Recognise him?'

And there he was. A much younger version — eighteen, perhaps — clean-shaven, unsmiling, staring straight at the camera with eyes that were empty of all emotion. It's strange the details you notice. His hair was longer, curlier. *Léon Solara*, said the caption.

Léon Solara. My Léon. I kept my eyes fixed on the photo. Léon's empty eyes stared back at me. The blood in my veins turned to ice.

20

For several seconds the only sound in the room was the quiet hum of the fridge in the corner and the tick, tick of the clock on the wall as the second hand edged forward. Falmire, and even Raymond, must have realised what an intense shock this was to me. Léon had lied — not in words, but in concealing his past from me.

I went over conversations I'd had with him — all the opportunities he'd had to speak up, to tell me that there was something about him I ought to know. The time when I asked had he ever thought of going to college, for example. He could have told me then. He could have said, *'Yes, actually, I wanted to go, but I was in prison.'*

Falmire took the tablet back from me without speaking. He searched for a short while until he found what he wanted.

'Here,' he said. 'You'll understand this. It's in French.' He placed the tablet in front of me and rose to his feet again. 'And now I think a strong cup of tea is called for.'

Raymond stood too, and began quietly clearing the table of the supper things. They were treating me with sympathy as if I'd suffered a bereavement. I would have seen the irony in my abductors showing a sensitive side, and found it amusing, if it weren't for the fact that my brain was frozen suddenly, and I could hardly think at all.

It seemed Léon — my Léon — had taken part in the robbery of a train in southern Italy. 'In an audacious theft,' the Montverrian article ran, 'in which hundreds of thousands of euros' worth of laptops and mobile phones were stolen, Léon Solara played a daredevil role. Video footage shows Solara dressed in black and with his face masked, breaking into a goods shed under cover of darkness. Here he proceeded to crawl under a freight train, where he waited patiently in the cold and dark for several hours.

'When daylight came, the train set off on its long journey from the port at Brindisi to its destination in Germany, with Solara in a dangerous position above one of the axles. The court heard that after travelling in this highly perilous way for more than an hour, Solara jumped down when the train stopped at a signal. Here, he forced open the door of one of the containers and climbed inside.'

I read on, filled with horror. I'd seen those long-distance freight trains hulking along the wide-gauge tracks in Italy. If he'd fallen under one of the wheels ... My fingers trembled, and I had to jab several times at the screen to scroll down the page. I read on.

The freight train had come to a halt again, this time in an unscheduled spot in an isolated location. The police later discovered the signals had been tampered with. Two large vans were ready and waiting. Several men jumped out, and Léon opened the door to the container. They then proceeded to throw boxes of high-tech equipment to each other and into the vans, the whole operation taking only a few minutes.

The article continued: 'For reasons unclear, Solara then made his way home alone, despite an arduous walk of more than twenty miles through countryside, until he reached the nearest train station.' According to the journalist, it was several weeks before any of the men were caught, but careless talk led the police to a warehouse on the west coast of Italy. It was filled with high-tech equipment stolen over several months from the railroad. With a sinking heart, I recognised the name of the town. It was near the place where Léon owned a house. Arrests followed rapidly, including that of the youth who'd concealed himself at great risk above the thundering wheels of the train. The police suspected mafia involvement in the heist, although nothing was proven.

'Because of his youth,' the article went on, 'and because this was his first offence, the judge reduced Solara's sentence to two years.' Two years. I scrolled back to the top of the screen and stared at Léon's photo. I should have felt something — anger that he'd lied, or even fear at the thought that I was caught up with a member of the Mafia. I was conscious only of a paralysing numbness.

Falmire gently removed the tablet and placed a mug of hot tea in its place. Then I realised that in the time I'd had the tablet in front of me, I could have used it to email for help, or put out a message on Twitter. I hadn't. I was too drained to care.

Falmire brought out a book from somewhere and began to read. Raymond played with his mobile phone, and I sat gazing ahead. As the hours passed, the numb sensation gradually lifted, and my brain began a slow whirl of thinking, thinking, thinking. Wondering what on earth I was going to do when all this was over.

21

The clock showed just after ten when the security monitor flickered into life, zooming in on a motorbike approaching the gate. I caught a glimpse of Léon's hand, clad in a leather glove, reaching over to press the buzzer.

Falmire rose and made his way to the intercom on the wall. He moved quickly, full of suppressed excitement. 'Léon,' he said, greeting him in his affable way. 'It's good of you to come. Do you have the diamond?'

The intercom crackled. 'Yes,' came the simple reply.

So he'd really stolen the diamond, and done it for my sake. A tsunami of violent emotions rose within me at the sound of his voice — joy at his arrival and that he was still safe; anger, horror and dismay at the past he'd concealed from me; fear of what was about to happen next. I rose to my feet, feeling like my heart might burst open.

The intercom crackled again. 'And Lizzie?'

'She's quite well,' Falmire said. 'Come inside and see for yourself.'

It was then I remembered the gun. I cast a swift glance at the counter and suffered a shock when I noticed it had gone. I turned sharply to where Raymond was standing in front of the monitor. His gaze was fixed on the screen, where Léon was listening to Falmire's instructions on where to go once he'd entered the grounds. There was a tell-tale bulge under Raymond's jacket.

I pushed back my chair and rushed to shout into the intercom. 'They've got a gun, Léon!' He turned his helmeted head towards the camera at the sound of my voice. It was impossible to see his expression, but his whole body seemed to stiffen.

'Would everyone please remain calm,' Falmire said, exasperated. 'I promise you there will be no shooting, and Elizabeth will come to no harm. All we want is the diamond.'

He pressed a button and the gates swung open. Léon accelerated through, and the gates closed behind him.

22

I cursed myself for not having attempted to take the gun before. I'd been so wrapped up in Falmire's revelations about Léon's past that I'd let the opportunity go by. *Stupid, stupid!* What was to stop Raymond shooting Léon dead as soon as he arrived?

Falmire was standing in front of the door, guarding it so I couldn't rush out to join Léon as soon as I heard him. My thoughts were in total disarray. Why hadn't I thought of an escape plan? I'd had all evening to do so, and now here I was, with Léon approaching what could turn out to be a deadly trap.

And then I heard the sound of his motorbike crunching over the gravel. Falmire faced the door, and I moved a few steps to one side, so that I was standing in front of Raymond and blocking his line of fire. It wasn't much of a plan, but it was the best I had. There were merely seconds remaining before Léon walked in, and my brain churned with possibilities. Should I turn and surprise Raymond by attempting to wrest the gun from him? When I'd seen women take on their attackers in films, it all seemed so easy. But Raymond had a hard, wiry body under his smart suit. What if he was quicker than me? What if I didn't succeed?

At that moment, just as I'd decided to risk everything with one desperate action, and just as Falmire's attention was occupied by opening the door, Raymond did something that astonished me. He lifted his hand, giving my shoulder a brief, sympathetic squeeze, almost making me leap in the air in the process. 'Don't worry,' he murmured in my ear. 'I won't shoot.' I caught a brief glimpse of his solemn, reassuring features, all trace of bored irony gone, before he stepped back — and then Falmire opened the door, and there was Léon.

'Léon!' I cried, rushing forward.

Raymond caught hold of my waist, pulling me back, so that I was held tightly against him. 'Don't move,' he murmured.

Léon's gaze found mine immediately. 'Lizzie. Are you all right?'

'Yes, don't worry. Everything's OK.'

Falmire stood between us, blocking Léon's path with his hand raised. 'A touching reunion,' he said. 'But before you're quite reunited, there's just the little matter of the diamond. Where is it?'

Léon removed one of his gloves and reached inside his leather jacket. For a heart-stopping moment I wondered if he, too, had a gun.

Raymond was on the alert. He let me go in a flash; and before I could react, his gun was pointing squarely at Léon.

Léon made no sign he'd noticed. He kept his eyes fixed on mine as he withdrew a small velvet bag from inside his jacket. He placed the bag on the kitchen table and pushed it towards Falmire with one finger. 'There's your diamond.'

Released from Raymond, I began to

edge around the table towards where Léon was standing near the open door. Falmire had forgotten everything else in the room, his attention occupied solely by the contents of the black bag. He loosened the ribbon at the bag's neck and withdrew the Scottish Diamond, holding it up so that it sparkled in the light.

'Home at last,' he murmured. There was a rapt smile on his face.

I reached Léon's side. He pulled me to him, making sure his body was between me and the gun in Raymond's hand.

'Take the fake,' Raymond told Léon, tilting his head sharply in the direction of the plastic box on the table, at the same time giving Léon a warning glance.

Léon scooped up the box and began to bundle me in the direction of the door. I looked at him in surprise. How did he know about the fake? Falmire hadn't mentioned it in any of his brief conversations with him.

But there was no time for questions. Léon propelled me up the steps, and then we were out in the blessed night, running towards his motorbike.

Falmire followed on our heels, coming to a halt on the doorstep. He lifted his hand in a wave. 'Goodbye, and thank you so much,' he said, just as though we were a couple of dinner guests. 'Don't forget what I told you, Elizabeth, about our friends the police.'

Léon passed me a crash helmet before mounting the bike, and I scrambled up behind him, putting on the helmet and fumbling with its fastenings at my chin.

'Goodbye, Elizabeth,' Falmire said again. 'Goodbye, Mr Solara.'

His last words were drowned in the roar of the engine. Léon turned the bike around, spraying gravel, and we raced down the drive, heading for the gate.

23

The night was pitch-black, and the air so cold the breath streamed from our mouths in great clouds. Within a few minutes of riding pillion, I was frozen to the bone. My pleated skirt and thin jacket were completely inadequate for a motorbike ride in a cold Scottish autumn, and I had no gloves. I wrapped my arms round Léon's waist, but in a short while I could barely feel the leather of his jacket under my fingers. I couldn't ride all the way back to Edinburgh like this without suffering from hypothermia.

I tugged on Léon's sleeve. 'Can we please stop?' I cried as loudly as I could above the rushing of the wind and the noise of the engine. 'I'm freezing!'

Léon barely glanced back at me. 'Soon!' he shouted.

He increased speed, and a blast of icy air whipped the hair around my neck and made the tips of my fingers burn with cold. I pressed my face against his back, trying to take shelter behind his broad shoulders from the freezing onrush. It was so unlike Léon — who was always considerate — not to stop when I asked. From the very first day I'd met him, his first thought had always been for my welfare. For Léon not to be concerned was unheard of.

I gripped his jacket. What on earth was going on in his mind? But what did I know, in any case? Léon Bressac was Léon Solara, and a completely different person to the one I'd thought I knew.

My shoulders ached with tension and I was shivering badly. Just when I thought I could carry on no longer, Léon decreased speed, coming to a halt in a layby in the middle of some woodland. In front of us was a dark blue van. And then the van's doors opened and there were men rushing towards us, silently and stealthily, from all sides. I sat rigid, paralysed with cold and fear.

Léon swung himself from the bike and

lifted me down, calling softly to one of the men in French: 'Quick, give me your coat.' Someone wrapped a dark overcoat around my shoulders. The scratchy fabric hung down below my knees. Léon put his arm around me.

'Tu as le diamant?' someone asked. 'Do you have the diamond?'

Léon ignored him. He pulled off his gloves and reached into my coat to take one of my frozen hands, sliding a glove first onto one and then the other of them. The blessed warmth was an immediate relief.

Two of the men from the van stepped up close. One of them had on a dark overcoat similar to the one I was shivering under. The other man was in his shirt sleeves. No doubt it was his coat I had around my shoulders. He smiled at me, his teeth a flash of white in the dark.

And then I recognised them. They were the two men from Montverrier who'd passed me on Calton Hill. And the man in the shirt sleeves had a gun in a holster. My teeth chattered, and I could barely think. Where had all these men come from? What was Léon doing here with them? Were we about to turn back to Helstone House? Were the Montverrians going to overpower Lord Falmire and wrest the Scottish Diamond from him?

'Your lady is brave,' the man in the shirt sleeves said with another flashing smile in my direction. I glared at him.

Léon squeezed my shoulder. 'Yes, she is.'

'Do you have the diamond?' the man wearing the coat asked impatiently. Again that question. What did they mean by it?

Léon reached inside his jacket and passed over the plastic box he'd picked up from Lord Falmire's table. The man with the coat opened the lid with the same rapt expression I'd seen on the face of Lord Falmire when Léon passed him the black velvet bag. In the dim light spilling out from inside the van, the Montverrian held the diamond aloft between a finger and thumb, and examined it carefully. It sparkled softly in his hand. He drew in a breath. '*Incroyable*,' he murmured.

Incredible.

The two Montverrian men began to speak in low voices, and the others in the group gathered round them, marvelling at the diamond's beauty. Through my chattering teeth I whispered to Léon, 'What's happening? Are they going to go back to Helstone House, to get the real diamond?' I began to feel a little afraid for Lord Falmire, alone in that enormous stately home with Raymond. These Montverrian men were no aristocratic amateurs. They looked like cold-blooded thugs. And like Raymond, at least one of them had a gun.

The man in the shirt sleeves lifted his head at my words and laughed softly. Then even the other one — the harsh-featured man in the overcoat — met my gaze with a look of amusement. I said to Léon, baffled, 'What's the joke?'

Léon's eyes glittered, hard and angry. 'It's no joke.' He indicated the jewel gleaming in the Montverrian man's hand. 'That one he's holding is the real diamond. Lord Falmire has the fake.'

146

The man in the dark overcoat said in English, in a thick, guttural accent, '*Fair is foul, and foul is fair.*' The group of men laughed quietly at his words.

I stared from one to the other, and back to Léon, and then at the diamond, glittering in the shadowy light. I'd seen Léon with my own eyes bring out the Scottish Diamond in a velvet bag and give it to Lord Falmire. Then I'd watched as he picked up the plastic box containing the fake and put it in his jacket. 'What sort of trick is this?' I asked.

Léon's hand was at my elbow, his face grim. 'Come. We've played our part, and you need to get in from the cold. Let's talk at home.'

The man in the overcoat placed the diamond back in its box and slipped it into his pocket. The group began to make their way on silent feet, back to their van. 'Come with us, Léon,' said the one in shirt sleeves, hanging back. 'There is room for you and your bike.' He indicated the open doors of the van and cast me a sympathetic look. 'And your girlfriend.

147

She looks cold.'

I had no intention of getting in their van with them. 'I'm warm enough — ' I began. At the same time, Léon said coldly, 'I'll take care of her.'

The Montverrian gave a slow, soft smile. With a hint of reluctant admiration, he said, 'You go your own way, as always, Léon.' He turned to me, his head slightly tilted, his smile turning to one of amusement. 'And my coat?'

I'd forgotten the coat. I began to take it off — I'd sooner have frozen to death on the road than get in that van with them — but Léon put his arm round my shoulders and pulled me to him. 'Lizzie needs the coat.'

Shirt-sleeves flicked a glance between us before raising his hands good-naturedly. 'Keep the coat,' he told me. His smile became one of regret. 'Goodbye, Léon. I'm sorry you won't join us.'

Léon said absolutely nothing. He held the other man's gaze, his eyes filled with an arctic chill such as I'd never witnessed in him before. I shivered inside my heavy coat.

The Montverrian raised his hands again, taking a few steps backwards. 'But no hard feelings,' he said, still with his smile. 'I hope our paths will cross again.' He gave me a pleasant nod. '*Au revoir*, Lizzie.' And then he climbed into the van. One of the group slid the door shut, the engine roared into life, and we watched the van disappear until the yellow glow from its headlights had completely vanished in the distance, and I was standing in the dark by the edge of an empty road, alone with a man called Léon Solara. My lover, and a stranger.

24

Léon handed me my helmet. I fumbled with the chin-strap with my gloved hands, and he took over, fastening it for me. His fingers were cold on the bare skin of my neck. When he'd finished, he raised his eyes to mine. The chill in them was gone — but what an emptiness had replaced the ice!

'Léon!' I reached out to place my hand on his arm, but he moved away to mount the bike.

'Time to go,' he said.

'At least take these.' I stripped off his gloves. 'I don't need them. My sleeves are so long. Look.' I waved my arms in the massive coat, making the sleeves flap about me like the wings of a crow.

At any other time, Léon might have smiled at the gesture. He put on the gloves without speaking. I climbed up behind him, and he started the engine.

Despite my thick coat, I very quickly began to feel the cold as we headed back to Edinburgh. The thought of a warm fire should have cheered me, but as we drew nearer and nearer home, my mind turned to the conversation that lay ahead, and a chill settled in my bones. Léon had hidden the truth from me. From now on nothing between us would ever be the same again.

It was almost midnight by the time we drew up outside my flat. Léon dropped me at the gate and watched me mount the steep steps, waiting with the engine running until I was safely inside before driving off to leave his bike in the garage. The flat was dark and cold, but the flames from the gas fire soon warmed the room. By the time Léon returned, the lamps were lit and I'd brought out a bottle of whisky and a couple of glasses.

He sank into an armchair by the fire and stretched out his legs, his movements stiff. I handed him a glass and sat in the chair opposite his. The whisky burned my throat and heated my belly, the warmth radiating through me. All the fear I'd felt earlier melted away, its place taken by a smouldering anger which I struggled to subdue.

I glanced at Léon. His face was pale, and there were dark rings under his eyes. 'Who has the real diamond?' I asked abruptly.

He lifted his gaze. '*Fair is foul and foul is fair,*' he quoted. There was a harshness in his voice I didn't recognise at all. He tossed down the remaining liquid in his glass. 'The Palace of Montverrier would be the ideal stage for your Scottish play,' he went on. 'A place filled with deception and greed. To answer your question, the diamond now with Lord Falmire at Helstone House — the one he believes to be real — is a fake. I put the real diamond in the hands of my colleagues from Montverrier. They arrived armed to receive it, in a secure van. I expect it's now under glass in the castle.'

'But *how*?' I said. 'I saw you give Lord Falmire the real diamond. It's not possible!'

'In Montverrier, anything is possible.' He reached for the whisky bottle, but I was before him. I poured us both another healthy measure and replaced the bottle on the floor between us.

'Let me explain to you how it was,' he continued, sinking his head back wearily. 'Although God knows it's a tale so full of twists and turns, it's enough to confound the most determined of listeners.'

I curled my feet under me, my frozen toes tingling as the warmth spread through them, and prepared to listen. And Léon began to tell me a tale that was so outlandish, it could only have happened in Montverrrier. And perhaps here in my home of Scotland too, where mystery and family dramas can stretch back for centuries and still seem as though they happened yesterday.

Léon swirled the liquid in his glass, frowning. 'Perhaps it would be best if I start right at the very beginning, from the time the diamond first came into the hands of the Montverrian royal family. You'll remember I told you about the

Jacobite revolution, and how Lord Falmire's ancestor lost the Scottish Diamond at cards?' I nodded, and he went on. 'Well, I discovered this evening from my Montverrian colleagues that Prince Sébastien was not the only person who cheated that night. Not long after he'd killed Lord Falmire in the duel, the prince discovered that the precious diamond he'd won at cards was actually a worthless fake.' Léon snorted. 'Ironic, really. Two guys playing cards — one of them cheats and the other stakes a fake diamond. And then they fight a duel over it.'

My eyes widened at this new piece of information. 'He'd pledged a fake? So where was the real diamond?'

'Well, that is the question that's been puzzling the Montverrian royal family for centuries. Until now. From what I discovered this evening, the truth of the real diamond's whereabouts was known only to the old Lord Falmire — and he was killed that night, taking his secret with him.' Léon gazed into his drink.

'The Montverrian royal family suspected for years afterwards that the real diamond had never even left Helstone House.'

'But — if they found out the diamond was a fake, why did they say nothing? They've been bringing the fake out in Montverrier for centuries, showing it off in full pomp. Why did they carry on pretending it was real?'

Léon curled his lip. 'Pride. The Montverrian people are full of it. Especially the royal family. They would have been determined not to lose face. And they could hardly go to the Falmire family and demand the real diamond, when Prince Sébastien had killed Lord Falmire in such dubious circumstances.

'And then a few years ago, apparently the present Lord Falmire travelled to Montverrier especially to see the diamond. He let slip to Princess Charlotte's father that he had found a fake diamond at his home in Scotland. A fake that looked so like the real thing, people would swear it was the original.'

I gave a gasp. Now it began to make

a little more sense. 'So after Lord Falmire's ancestor was killed in the duel, the Falmire family must have believed what everyone else thought — that the real diamond had been lost at cards in Montverrier.' I pondered this for a while and then added, 'And I suppose even if the family really had known that Lord Falmire had staked a false diamond, in those days they would never have spoken of it. It would have been far too shameful.' I frowned, trying to piece together a likely sequence of events, but after three hundred years it was impossible to know exactly what could have taken place, or why the real diamond had been forgotten.

Léon chimed in with my thoughts. 'We can only speculate. One thing's for sure — if the Montverrian royal family kept bringing out the fake for official ceremonies, and they never once revealed the truth, it's not surprising future generations of Falmires believed them. Why would they doubt it?'

'They certainly forgot about their own diamond. Falmire told me he found it left by some child inside a doll's house in the nursery. It seems generations of children had been playing with it like a toy.'

Léon gave a low whistle. 'What a lucky chance. It could so easily have been thrown away. And when Falmire told Princess Charlotte's father that he'd come across a diamond in Scotland, the king guessed immediately that it was the real gemstone. He became determined to get it into his possession, by fair means or foul.'

What a fantastical story. If it had concerned anyone else, I would never have believed it, but by now I could believe the Montverrian royal family capable of anything. And the Scottish Falmires, too.

'But then when the king became ill,' Léon continued, 'Princess Charlotte made it her business to carry out her father's plan on his behalf.'

And then the penny finally dropped. 'So that's why she decided to exhibit her diamond in Edinburgh Castle!' I exclaimed. 'It was all part of a plan to draw Lord Falmire out, and to trap him into giving up the real diamond, right from the very beginning!'

'Correct again.' Léon shifted his legs and rested his glass on the arm of his chair. 'I don't believe the princess knew exactly how the exchange could be accomplished, even after the exhibition was all arranged. But the Montverrians love a gamble. They decided to take a chance that something might happen. Some small opportunity might arise that they could seize on and bend in their favour. After all, they had nothing to lose. And this is where Raymond comes in.'

And then Léon began to tell me everything that had happened after he'd discovered I'd been abducted, laying bare an astonishing sequence of events. When he heard me shout out in the car as I was being driven away, his immediate thought was to come chasing straight after me. But Léon has always been cool-headed. A couple of moments' reflection was enough for him to decide, reluctantly, that his best option would be to enlist the help of the Montverrian men at the castle. Those men are tough, and they're resourceful. With their back-up, he would be more certain of rescuing me unharmed. At that time, too, he had no idea the Scottish Diamond he was guarding was a fake. He had no intention of stealing it — he fully intended to rescue me without it. And so he went straight back to the castle to meet with the Montverrians — and straight into the fog of deceit that awaited him.

'It was then they told me I needn't worry about taking the diamond. That it was a fake. And then I had my second unpleasant shock of the evening.' Léon's eyes narrowed to two slits of glittering ice. 'They already knew of your abduction. And in fact, they'd been behind it.'

My head shot up at this, and a few drops of whisky leaped out of my glass. I fixed my astounded gaze on Léon. 'What? Are you seriously saying your Montverrians planned my abduction? But how? And why on earth … ?'

'You were the opportunity that came along, and the bait they seized. When I first approached them that day in the courtyard at the castle, they told me their security guard Raymond had gone missing. They lied to me. They knew exactly where Raymond was. He was in contact with them the whole time.'

'*Raymond?*' With every sentence Léon uttered, I felt I was walking further and further into a murky mist. 'But — Raymond has been stalking me for weeks; you know it. Waiting outside the rehearsal studio and following me on the street. He's been dogging my every move. Raymond's in league with Falmire. He's Falmire's *boyfriend.*'

Léon looked up from the fire and his eyes met mine, the irises shining with a brief flash of fury, like two points of flame. 'Raymond might be Falmire's boyfriend, but he's double-crossing him. He works for Princess Charlotte.' His voice, usually so calm and measured, vibrated with anger. 'Raymond's sole aim in coming to Scotland was to befriend Lord Falmire.'

My body was exhausted, but my mind darted round and round in circles. It was no wonder everything was shrouded in fog. Wherever the princess went, deception and trickery surrounded her. *'Fair is foul and foul is fair ...'* I'd been hearing those words in my nightmares ever since we began rehearsing our cursed play. I thought of the way the men from Montverrier had appeared out of the mist that evening, like a band of diabolical conspirators. If ever there was a country shrouded in intrigue ...

'What a tale of treachery,' I said. 'Raymond is actually employed by Princess Charlotte, and he's double-crossing Lord Falmire. What I don't understand is, why was Raymond following me? And why did the Montverrians not tell you what was going on right from the start? Why keep it all a secret?'

'They kept it a secret because I'm not one of them. When I approached them in the castle grounds that time, looking for a job, they must have thought me a complete fool. A gift from the gods.' His dark gaze was fixed on the liquid in his glass, his jaw clenched.

'Hey,' I said gently. 'They lied to you. They've been practising trickery for thousands of years. What chance do we have against people like that? Don't even think of blaming yourself.'

'I should have realised they had something crooked going on. If I hadn't been so desperate for a job ... ' He closed his eyes, pinching the bridge of his nose. 'I discovered that before the fake diamond even left Montverrier, Raymond had made a point of seeking out Lord Falmire and befriending him. He knew the sorts of bars and clubs Falmire went to. It was easy enough to single him out and strike up a conversation.'

'But — ' I stopped right there. Raymond was a good-looking young man with a wiry, muscular build that would easily attract attention. As Jeannie had pointed out to me several times, Raymond was 'cute'. He could also be perfectly charming, too, if he wanted to play that role. It was easy to see how Lord Falmire must have been led on by him.

'And so Lord Falmire was duped,' I

162

said. 'I could almost feel sorry for him.'

Léon looked up swiftly at that. 'Yes, Falmire was duped. He was also greedy; and, worst of all, he embroiled you in a plot with armed men and put your life at risk. If I had hold of him now … ' He broke off, his hand gripping his glass so tightly I thought it might shatter. The hot anger I'd seen blaze out of his eyes a few moments before had been replaced with a lethal ice. I reached forward to touch his hand, but before I could do so he rose to his feet in one swift movement, draining his whisky as he did so. He placed the empty glass on the table beside him and looked down at me.

'So perhaps now you can piece the rest together,' he said. 'The Montverrians decided to employ me, and their plot came together when they realised I had a girlfriend. You. That's when they saw their chance. From then on, Raymond began to fill Lord Falmire's head with the idea that the diamond in the castle was rightfully his, and that he knew a way to get it back. He told Falmire all he had to do was invent an excuse to get you in the car, and he'd do the rest.'

I uncurled my legs from under me and stood, looking up into Léon's dark gaze. 'The mist has cleared a little,' I said. 'Or as much as it ever will do. The Montverrians took a chance, and Raymond engineered my abduction. I wonder if those two men saw you that day on Calton Hill? I'm sure I heard one of them say your name. Léon Bressac.'

'It's possible.' Léon gave a tired shrug. 'But what does it matter now?' He drew in a small breath, making no move to touch me; but his eyes, gazing into mine, softened. 'You're safe now,' he said quietly. 'And that's all that matters.'

I would have given anything, then, to have reached up and kissed him, and felt his familiar arms around me, warm and strong, and let that be the end of our adventure. But I didn't move. The distance remained between us. Léon's eyes clouded as he waited for me to speak. And then I asked the one question that really mattered in all of this.

'Who is Léon Solara?'

25

Léon's face paled. The shadows under his eyes stood out in dark relief, and he had the exhausted look of a boxer who has gone into the ring and given everything he has and come out defeated. He gave an infinitesimal, resigned nod, as though acknowledging his fight was over. 'I'm guessing it was Raymond who told you.'

'Lord Falmire told me. He thought he could use your criminal record as a weapon. Although it must have been Raymond who first told Falmire of it.'

Léon reached out as though to touch me, but thought better of it. He dropped his hand to his side and moved to the window, where he stood with his back to me, looking out. His shoulders had lost their usual straightness. Wearily, he pressed his forehead against the glass.

'My name is Léon Bressac, after my father,' he began. 'But in Italy, I took my mother's name of Solara. I was eighteen, living with my mother in the house I now own by the sea. We had moved there from Rome because my mother was ill. Terminally ill. She had leukaemia and had been ill for a very long while. What little savings she possessed dwindled very quickly, and so I left school to get a job to support us both. It was difficult. I was working at a mechanic's, but my mother needed care at home, and I couldn't manage to be in two places at once. The authorities said they would take her into a care home to die, but — '

He broke off, raising a hand and pressing it to the glass, as though it might steady him. Although his back was to me, I saw his reflection in the window. His face was cold as ashes, but when he continued speaking, his voice was firm. 'The thought of my mother dying among strangers was unbearable to me. But what could I do? And then I was approached by some men in Italy. Friends of friends of people I knew in Montverrier. They were looking for someone young and fit for a job. They would pay well. They mentioned a figure that seemed astronomical to me. They said it would be regular work. Of course when they told me what it was, I hesitated; but to be perfectly honest with you — '

He broke off again, perhaps recognising the irony of his words. Then he repeated, 'To be honest with you, I didn't hesitate for long. I intended to do the job once, take the money offered and never have anything more to do with them.'

I set my glass on the table next to Léon's and sank back down into my chair. The warming effect of the whisky had long since evaporated, leaving a chill in its wake. I wrapped my arms around myself. 'When you first saw those men from Montverrier in the courtyard at Edinburgh Castle,' I said, gazing at Léon's back, 'you told me they recognised you, because everybody knows everybody in Montverrier. But that wasn't the case, was it? They recognised you from the time you stole from the train.'

In the window, Léon's reflection gazed back at me, dark-eyed, as though he were outside the room looking in. He nodded. 'Some of those Montverrian men — the man who gave you his coat, for example — have connections with the gang in Italy. That's how they recognised me.'

'Oh, Léon, Léon,' I said in a half-whisper. 'Why didn't you tell me? Couldn't you trust me?'

'If I'd told you I'd been in prison when we first met — or during those weeks we spent in the Palace of Montverrier — what would you have thought of me? You ran away from me then, even without knowing the truth; so what if I'd told you I was a thief and a convicted criminal? You would never have trusted me.'

I thought back to that time — to the weeks we'd spent alone together in the princess's suite, when the treachery that surrounded me in Montverrier had come to light. Léon was right; I'd assumed he was a part of the deception. I'd failed to trust him, and I'd run away.

There was nothing I could say now, and my lack of response must have told Léon everything he needed to know.

The silence stretched between us. I remembered the emptiness I'd witnessed in Léon's expression over the past few weeks, and I finally understood his desolation. A similar wretchedness settled deep within me. I shivered.

Léon turned. 'It's late, Lizzie. Time to sleep.' He moved away from the window to return to the armchair opposite mine, where he stretched out his legs and sank back, his hands resting lightly on the arms of the chair.

I was drained, yet my thoughts refused to stop their wild dance. I stole a glance at Léon's exhausted features and asked tentatively, 'And your mother? Did you get your wish for her to die at home?'

Léon's hands gripped the arms of the chair once, then relaxed. His eyes remained fixed on the fire. 'My mother died while I was in prison,' he said carefully. 'In a care home. There was no one else to look after her.'

'Oh, Léon.' My tired eyes filled with tears, spilling over in a quick, hot rush. I rose swiftly to take one of the hands that rested on the chair, and I kissed it. 'I'm so sorry, Léon.' I dropped down to sit on the rug beside him, my back against his chair, my cheek resting against his knee, and began to weep.

His hand touched my hair. 'Don't cry,' he said softly.

But it was no use. My chest rose and fell with sobs while his warm hand caressed my hair. I have no idea how long we sat there. The sounds of the city below grew silent, and the night sky grew darker still before the dawn. All Léon's sorrow seemed to flow from him into me, as though we were one, and the pain was suffered equally by both of us.

Finally my tears dried, as though their well was exhausted. In the warmth of the fire, and under the soothing touch of Léon's hand, my head began to droop. I tried to rouse myself, but in the end, exhaustion won.

When I opened my eyes again, I was lying alone on the rug beside the fire, with a cushion pillowed under my head and a blanket tucked around me. Daylight was filtering through the window, pooling in warm patches on the floorboards. I stretched my cramped limbs and sat up. Léon's chair was empty. I listened, head to one side. The flat was completely silent.

26

I scrambled to my feet, alert and completely awake. I knew, without even searching for him, that Léon had left; and I was hit by that same certainty of my love for him that had struck me so forcefully in Falmire's car. In the overwhelming emptiness of my flat, I suffered a moment of intense pain, as though a hand had plucked my heart from my ribcage and crushed it in one swift movement.

I started towards the door, not knowing what to do, except perhaps throw on my coat and rush out to Léon's garage to see if I could find him there. But before I'd taken two paces, I noticed the piece of paper lying on the table where I did my work. I picked it up with shaking hands.

My dearest Lizzie ... Léon's careful handwriting swam in front of my eyes. I moved to the window, where the morning sun shed light over his words ... *I* love you more than my heart can bear. I had hoped for so many things from a life with you. Such dreams I had — the beauty of them shone pure and clear in my mind when I looked to the future, like the brightest star. But like the mention of your Scottish play, I have brought you only bad luck. My own broken soul was never fit for such goodness. It was stupid of me ever to think it. I want only the best things for you, my lovely Lizzie, and I am no good. Since my release, I have tried many times to start again. There was the job I told you of in Switzerland, where I acted as bodyguard to a wealthy family's children. My employers learned of my conviction in Italy, and told me — with regret — that they would have to let me go. The children cried when I left. In the end, I brought them only sorrow, as I have done you. The sight of your tears is a torture. The bank, and all the other places I tried to find work in Scotland, have refused me. And who can blame them? No one will employ a thief. No one, it seems, except my countrymen *from Montverrier, and after today I will never take employment from them again. I am going back to Italy, to decide what to do with my future. You have been the one true and good thing to appear in my life since I was set free. If there is ever a time I can help you, now or in the future, send me word and I will come to you. My heart is yours, my sweet, kind, precious, beautiful Lizzie, and I wish you a life filled with all the happiness I am not able to give you. Léon.*

I let the letter fall and raced to the hall, where I ran out of the front door, leaving it wide open. The cold morning air cut through my thin blouse. I pounded down the steps and downhill, all along the Grassmarket and through a covered alleyway, panting and stumbling until I reached the cobbled street and Léon's garage.

The steel shutter was drawn down. I rattled and rattled on the cold metal, calling his name. No one answered.

27

Three days later, I boarded a plane to Naples. For the whole three days I carried Léon's letter with me always, reading his words so often I knew them by heart. He loved me. That knowledge filled me with a hope as bright and clear as his own dreams had once been. I felt such impatience to see him, I would have left Edinburgh the very day I found his letter, but rushing would have solved nothing. If Léon were travelling across Europe by bike, it would take him several days, and there was no point in arriving at his house before he did. Besides, there was the important consideration of my theatre. I couldn't possibly let the other cast members down just as we were about to put on our first performance of *Macbeth*. It was the longest three days of my life.

By the time I boarded the plane, my heart and mind were filled with a wild mixture of elation and trepidation. I gazed out of the window at the clouds floating by beneath me, and the final speech from *Macbeth* entered my mind, with Malcolm's promise to '*call home our exiled friends abroad*'. I thought of Léon, and his self-imposed exile, and my eyes filled with tears.

If willpower alone could move an aircraft, we would have arrived in Naples in minutes rather than hours, but at last the plane came to a halt and the doors opened. I stepped onto the concourse with relief, the welcome heat warming my Scottish bones. The sun's rays bounced brightly from every surface. I shaded my eyes and strode into the airport building, hurrying through passport control, straight past the baggage carousel and out through customs. I'd brought only a small carry-on bag. Whatever happened, in twenty-four hours I would be returning to Edinburgh — either with Léon, or without him.

Outside the airport, I approached one of the waiting taxis. I don't speak much

Italian, and Léon's house is hard to find, hidden as it is on a narrow track overlooking the sea. I showed the driver the map I'd saved to the screen of my phone. His reply was incomprehensible, but since he smiled and nodded and put his finger and thumb together in a gesture to show he understood, I climbed inside.

I discovered I'd arrived in the right country for someone who was in love and impatient. There is never a need to ask a Neapolitan taxi driver to hurry. We drove at a satisfying speed out of the airport, and soon we were heading past the city of Naples towards the sea. It wasn't long before we came upon the coast road I'd driven down with Léon in the summer. The same stone houses, bleached by the sun, tumbled down to the sea, shining turquoise beneath us. I'd forgotten the astonishing sight of it. How could I persuade Léon to leave this wonderful heat and the beauty of the Italian coast? The only thing waiting for him in Edinburgh was my cold flat, and the start of a damp Scottish winter.

By the time the taxi driver left the main road to begin edging down the narrow track to Léon's house, I was convinced I'd made a terrible mistake, and I was about to make an embarrassing fool of myself. I stepped out of the car and pulled out some euros to pay the driver. Something of my wretchedness must have shown in my face. He patted my hand in a fatherly way. '*In bocca al lupo*,' he said, with a reassuring smile. In the mouth of the wolf. I remembered what Léon had told me about how to say good luck in Italian, the night I'd worried over the superstition surrounding *Macbeth*. My spirits rose, and I answered the driver firmly, '*Crepi il lupo.*' To hell with the wolf. He grinned and lifted his thumb.

The engine started up, and he began to reverse at a dangerous speed back down the track. The cloud of dust the car left in its wake settled, a couple of gulls flew back down to resume their desultory pecking in the grit, and I was alone. I stood outside the blue painted door of Léon's house. All was quiet.

For a moment or two, my heart sank. I thought perhaps he hadn't arrived home yet. I almost turned to run back down the track, hoping I might be in time to stop the taxi driver. But then I recognised the signs that the house was occupied. The veranda had been neatly swept of dust, and the profuse bougainvillea blooming over the doorway had been recently trimmed. The heady scent of its purple blossom drifted towards me as I gave a light rap on the door. No answer.

I peered through the window to find the kitchen was empty. A loaf of bread, standing on the table beside an empty coffee cup, was further proof that Léon was home. I hid my bag around the side of the house, where no one could see it, and set off down the rocky, twisting steps cut into the hillside, to the place I was sure to find him.

28

The sun's rays struck the surface of the sea with a glorious flickering light. At the bottom of the steps, I took off my white sandals and, with the warm, gritty sand beneath my feet, I began to make my way along the beach. The tiny bay below Léon's house is circled by great dry cliffs, and I had the feeling as I walked along that I was in the middle of a Roman amphitheatre.

I was filled with the same sensation I have just before going on stage — anticipation mixed with excitement and fear. I came to a halt and scanned the sea, shading my eyes. And then I saw him in the distance, his dark arms rising and falling, cutting through the turquoise and gold in glittering strokes. I made my way a little further until I came upon his towel and his pile of clothes neatly folded on the sand, beside an open paperback. I sat down with my back against the warm rock face and waited. I didn't have to wait long.

Perhaps the excited chatter of the gulls alerted him, or else he'd made out my figure as I'd stood at the sea's edge, looking out for him. He turned and headed for the shore. When he reached shallow waters, he stood, a silhouette against the shimmering blue. The sun was behind him. I couldn't make out his expression, but as he stepped out of the sea and made his way towards me, shedding drops of golden water, I had the impression of a person radiating joy.

I stood to greet him. All the words I'd prepared took flight at the sight of him, like a flock of starlings. It seemed Léon was equally tongue-tied. He bent to pick up his towel and began to rub his hair and torso, the tattoo of a bird on his arm rising and falling with his movements. I tore my gaze from him and turned my attention to the shimmering sea.

'There are some things I wanted to say to you,' I blurted out as he continued to towel himself. 'That's why I've come.'

Léon said, in his usual calm way, 'I'm very happy to see you.' He bent to spread out his shirt on the sand for me. 'Sit down.'

I arranged myself on his warm shirt, legs bent, hugging my knees. Léon stretched his sun-browned legs in front of him and leaned back against the cliff. His warm skin smelled of the sea. Although he'd barely spoken, I had the impression still that he was filled with a pent-up joy. I, too, was bursting with rapture. The shining sea, the warmth, and above all, Léon beside me made it almost impossible to organise my thoughts. I tried to calm the fluttering starlings, keeping my gaze away from his warm, damp limbs and resolutely on the waves.

'I wanted to tell you how sorry I am about everything,' I said, my words tumbling out. 'I'm sorry I didn't trust you when we were in Montverrier, and I'm sorry you couldn't trust me in Edinburgh. I'm so sorry about everything that happened to you, about your mum, and about everything that happened afterwards. It's made me very sad to think about it.'

Léon rested a hand on the sand beside me. I knew him well enough by now to know he was waiting patiently until I'd completely finished, before he himself would speak. I picked up a handful of the hot sand and let it trickle through my fingers. 'When I saw you so miserable in Edinburgh, I thought it was because you couldn't fit in in a strange country, and because you missed home. I even thought it might be because you'd stopped loving me, and regretted coming.'

Léon shifted at that, but I turned, putting my hand over his on the sand. 'I understand now,' I said, the joy filling me again. 'I realised I was wrong when I read your letter. And I've come here to ask you something, and I really, really hope you'll say yes to it.' I drew in a breath. 'I know why it was so hard for you to find work, but I've had an idea. I love the way you tell stories. If you carried that through on the stage, you could have audiences eating out of your hand. I thought ... '

184

Another quick breath, and then I said in a rush, 'I thought I'd ask you if you'd like to join our theatre. As an actor, I mean.'

I threw him a quick glance, but his eyes were lowered, and his expression unreadable. 'It doesn't pay much,' I went on when he didn't answer. 'We none of us earn a lot. But we love it. And another thing is, we often visit young offenders' institutes, and I thought — if you didn't mind it — you could speak to the young people there about your own experiences, and it might help them see they could have a future.'

Léon drew his hand out from under mine and replaced it on his knee. 'I see,' he said slowly. I looked at him, and all my bright hope began to dwindle when I realised his own joy had faded. He drew up his legs and leaned forward, his hands resting loosely on his knees. 'So you've come here to ask me if I'd like a job.'

'Yes.' And then I realised — *stupid!* — just why he looked so downcast. I got to my knees swiftly and leaned towards him, taking his face in my hands. 'But not just that. I don't care if you don't want to work with me. I didn't come here just to offer you a job. I came here to tell you I don't care about anything except not losing you like this again. I wanted to tell you just how much I love you. I don't want to live without you, and if — if you can't bear to live in Scotland, then I'll even come and live here' A pause. 'That is, if you still love me.'

The light that had dimmed in Léon's eyes glowed brightly. His solemn, teasing gaze met mine. 'If I still love you?' My dearest Lizzie, you have no idea how much. Even enough to come to Scotland, with your dar-r-r-k super-r-r-rstitions and your cold and rain. I'd love more than anything to be a part of your theatre. It would make me the happiest man in the world.'

He put his hands around my waist and guided me down onto the sand, leaning over me so his body blocked the sun, his eyes shining as bright as the sea. 'On one condition,' he added.

My happiness wavered. 'What's that?'

'No more *Macbeth*.'

I laughed, and then he bent and kissed me, and my heart soared with such joy, I thought it might burst from my body and float up to join the glorious sun.

We do hope that you have enjoyed reading this large print book.

Did you know that all of our titles are available for purchase?

We publish a wide range of high quality large print books including:
Romances, Mysteries, Classics
General Fiction
Non Fiction and Westerns

Special interest titles available in large print are:
The Little Oxford Dictionary
Music Book, Song Book
Hymn Book, Service Book

Also available from us courtesy of Oxford University Press:
Young Readers' Dictionary
(large print edition)
Young Readers' Thesaurus
(large print edition)

For further information or a free brochure, please contact us at:
Ulverscroft Large Print Books Ltd.,
The Green, Bradgate Road, Anstey,
Leicester, LE7 7FU, England.
Tel: (00 44) **0116 236 4325**
Fax: (00 44) **0116 234 0205**

Other titles in the
Linford Romance Library:

HEART OF THE MOUNTAIN

Carol MacLean

Emotionally burned out from her job as a nurse, Beth leaves London for the Scottish Highlands and the peace of her aunt's cottage. Here she meets Alex, a man who is determined to live life to the full after the death of his fiancée in a climbing accident. Despite her wish for a quiet life, Beth is pulled into a friendship with Alex's sister, bubbly Sarah-Jayne, and finds herself increasingly drawn to Alex . . .

MIDSUMMER MAGIC

Rebecca Bennett

Fearing that her ex-husband plans to take their daughter away with him to New Zealand, Lauren escapes with little Amy to the remote Cornish cottage bequeathed to her by her Great-aunt Hilda. But Lauren had not even been aware of Hilda's existence until now, so why was the house left to her and not local schoolteacher Adam Poldean, who seemed to be Hilda's only friend? Lauren sets out to learn the answers — and finds herself becoming attracted to the handsome Adam as well.

DANGEROUS WATERS

Sheila Daglish

On holiday in the enchanting Hungarian village of Szentendre, schoolteacher Cassandra Sutherland meets handsome local artist Matthias Benedek, and soon both are swept up in a romance as dreamy as the moon on the Danube. But Matt is hiding secrets from Cass, and she is determined never to love another man like her late fiance, whose knack for getting into dangerous situations was the ruin of them both. Can love conquer all once it's time for Cass to return home to London?

THE MAGIC OF THORN HOUSE

Christina Green

After the death of her dear Aunt Jem, Carla Marshall inherits Thorn House, the ancient country manor where she spent a happy childhood. But her arrival brings with it fresh problems. She meets and falls in love with local bookseller Dan Eastern — but is he only after the long-lost manuscript of one of Aunt Jem's books, which would net him a fortune if Carla can find it? And her aunt's Memory Box hides a secret that's about to turn Carla's world upside down . . .